PhotoJENic

Wendy Bruening

All for Him

CHAPTER ONE

L adies and gentlemen, if you'll please join me on this side of the room, the bride and groom are about to cut their wedding cake." The DJ's voice flooded the reception hall.

Guests got up from their dinner tables and made their way towards the corner of the room. Before long, a crowd formed around a small table. In its center was the focus of the entire group, the bride and groom with their sugary, tiered confection.

With an oversized knife in hand, they stood poised, ready to slice. The bride guided the groom's hand, and together they cut and removed a piece of cake.

Onlookers talked amongst themselves. An eager, middle-aged woman craned her neck to catch a glimpse of the couple. "Do you think they'll smash it?"

The woman next to her clapped her hands together with excitement. "Oh, looks like he's thinking about it."

A small sea of phone screens waited in the air, prepared to capture the picture at any moment.

Hesitantly, the bride and groom took a bite-sized morsel and lifted it to their spouse's face. The bride bit down on her lip in nervous anticipation, as the groom playfully put a dot of butter cream on her nose. Giggling, they fed each other the first taste of cake.

Applause and cheers erupted from the group.

STOP! Right there — This was Jen's favorite part of any wedding. *What are they gonna do with the left over frosting on their fingers?* In her opinion, it was the most realistic moment of the day; just two ordinary people, with icing on their fingers and crumbs on their faces. In Jen's mind, what a couple did in that kind of situation said more about them than any song, or flower arrangement they had chosen for the event.

Jen pressed the shutter button just as the groom gave his new wife a napkin and then moved in for a quick kiss. She breathed a contented sigh as she gazed at the couple.

After the cake-cutting event, Jen made her way back across the room toward the DJ booth and staff dining table.

Weaving her way between tables, she snapped pictures of chatting pairs, and dancing guests. *The Ivy Manor is filled with quite a trendy bunch tonight. This couple's really into having whatever is popular right now.* She'd keep that in mind while editing their pictures in the coming week.

Jen shouted over the music to the large, balding

man in a tuxedo, standing behind the speakers. "Hey, Al."

Al was adjusting the playlist on his laptop. Looking up he gave Jen a toothy grin. "Hi Jen. How's the group been for ya so far today? Seems like we might have a rowdy bunch on our hands tonight." He gestured with a chubby hand toward the crowd of dancing guests.

"So far, so good." Jen paused to photograph a couple of twenty-something frat boy types, who danced under Al's flashing, rainbow light show. "Looks like the couple went for Big Al's Deluxe Entertainment Package, huh?"

"Yep. They wanted it all—projection screen, photo booth, additional lighting. All of which I was happy to provide, of course." Grinning, he rubbed his hands together. When the song ended Big Al spoke to the crowd, "All right, everyone. Let's slow it down with a couple of classics."

A woman's soulful voice poured from the speakers and filled the room. Men and women pulled each other close, as the famous love song played.

Once Jen had captured a few romantic photographs, she returned to her conversation with the DJ. "So, is Carol looking forward to your cruise?" Jen leaned against the wall, swept her long blonde hair to one side of her face, and began to twist it in her hands, away from the camera's strap around her neck.

"Ya know, it's still a month away, and my wife is already packing." Al shook his head and chuckled. "I'd be lying if I said I didn't love her enthusiasm. Did I tell ya, because of that trip, we'll be away for three weekends? I've enlisted Nate, Carol's nephew, to run the show for me the days I'll be away. He did quite a bit of work for me before my brother and I bought the Ivy Manor. In fact, he's on his way here for some on the job refreshers."

At that moment, a tall, dark haired man in his mid-twenties stepped behind Al and slapped him on the back. "Hi, Uncle Al!" He beamed and gave his relative a hearty handshake.

"Nate. Speak of the devil. We were just talking about you." He turned toward Jen. "Jen, this is my nephew, Nate. Nate, this is Jen. She's the resident photographer around here."

The music changed, and a male singer took over with another standard.

Nate took Jen's hand in both of his and shook it. "Nice to meet you."

"Same here." A friendly smile spread across her face. "I've been told you'll be helping out for a while."

"That's the plan," Nate shrugged. "So, what about you? How'd you get roped into spending your weekends with this guy?" He jabbed a thumb in his uncle's direction.

Jen laughed. "Well, after Al and Frankie bought the Ivy Manor, they decided to offer their customers a full line of wedding services. Frankie was already providing the catering, and Al was the DJ part of things. Anyway, Al saw me shoot different weddings, then, since we were getting along so well, they asked if I'd like to work with them. The rest is history."

"Sounds like you've got a pretty good gig going."

"Yeah, I really like it. Speaking of which, if I want to keep it, I should probably take some pictures." Jen lifted the camera hanging around her neck. "It was nice talking to you."

"You, too." Nate smiled. "I'll catch you next weekend, if you're around."

"Looking forward to it," Jen called over her shoulder as she made her way toward the dance floor.

A crowd-pleasing, hip-hop video flashed on the projection screen, and Big Al called out in his best DJ voice, "Gather 'round all you single ladies, it's time for the bouquet toss."

* * * * *

Later that night, Jen pulled her beat-up white sedan into a parking space in front of her apartment building. Exhausted after the long day of work, she dragged her camera bag, and as much equipment as she could carry in one trip, out of the trunk.

The straps of her equipment bags dug into her shoulders and weighed her down. Unlocking the door to the building, she then made her way up six flights of stairs. With every step, her feet ached in her high heeled boots. After opening the door of her apartment, Jen trudged down the hall, trying not to wake her roommate. Entering her bedroom, she dropped everything into her closet. Then with her last bit of energy, she pulled off her boots and changed into a pair of sweats, immediately collapsing on her pillow top mattress and falling asleep.

CHAPTER TWO

Beep... Beep... Beep... Beep...
Oh goodness, it can't be morning already. Jen fumbled around the nightstand, trying to find the button that would relieve her ears from the horrendous, early morning assault. Finally, she found and hit the snooze. *Ah, sweet relief. It's Monday already.* She let out a groan. *Where did the weekend go?* Jen rolled her head from side to side to relieve the ache in her neck. Her right wrist hurt from the way she tended to hold her camera with her hand bent backwards while she wasn't taking pictures. Her feet throbbed from spending the weekend in heels. She'd do anything to get a perfect shot and that included running, climbing, or crouching.

As tired as she was, the thought of listening to her alarm again, paired with the desire for a long hot shower, was enough to get her out of bed.

When she stepped out of the bathroom, the aroma of freshly brewed coffee filled her nose.

"Morning, Claire," Jen called. Tying her robe, she made her way down the short hallway to the kitchen.

"Morning. I made coffee." Claire took a mug from the cabinet and poured a cup for her roommate.

"Hey, you changed your hair!" Jen paused and looked her friend up and down. "And you're awfully dressed up, for work. Are those new clothes?"

"They sure are." Claire spun around, showing off her ensemble. A dark pencil skirt, crisp white shirt, and sling back heels dressed her tiny frame. Her short, shocking pink hair flared as she twirled. "After the date I had yesterday, I needed a pick me up."

The pair had been best friends since high school. While Jen generally considered her roommate to be quite level headed and mature, when it came to dating, Claire was simply man crazy. As a chemist, she was often cooped up in a lab filled with white-haired, old men. As a result, she jumped at every opportunity to be around people of her own age. Her job, and the men in her life, seemed to cause Claire's ever-changing hair color. She'd said it was her way of de-stressing. Some people shop and some people vent, but Claire dyed her hair.

Jen cringed. "That bad, huh?"

"Worse than you can imagine." Claire sighed and shook her head. "I'll tell you all about it after work. We still on for girl night?"

Jen picked up her cup. "Definitely."

"Good. The only thing that's going to get me through this day is the thought of vegging on the couch for hours." Claire drank the last sip of her coffee and placed the mug in the sink. "I'll see you tonight." Grabbing her coat, she then headed for the door.

"Bye," Jen called. "Okay, time to get myself in gear," she spoke aloud, in an attempt to motivate herself.

After selecting an album from her docked mp3 player, she clicked play and meandered down the hall to finish dressing. Once her locks were blow-dried, she pulled them into a ponytail, selected a pair of jeans and a warm hoodie to wear, and then made her way to her desk.

Their apartment was perfect for the two women. The kitchen and living room were just one space, giving the small home a much bigger feel. They filled the area with mismatched pieces of furniture, rugs, throw pillows, and blankets; the collection had been acquired from various flea markets, craft boutiques, or Jen's parents. Together they created a cozy, eclectic feel, an appearance that both Jen and Claire loved.

The backdrop for it all was the large set of windows that each day delivered a gorgeous view of Lake Erie.

Jen turned on her computer, then plopped down in her office chair. While she waited for it to boot up, she took in the view. When they first moved in, Claire, knowing that her friend couldn't stand to work in small dark rooms, insisted that Jen's desk be placed directly under the windows. With the desk the focal point of the room, the rest of their things were arranged around it. Almost two years later, Jen was still thankful that that's where she got to do her picture editing each day.

Being that it was late March, the lake was in nearly the same state it had been since the previous November. Frozen blocks of ice had piled up on the shore. Dirt and gravel had also found a home along the muddy, gray, water. Today, however, the usually monotone sky had the slightest hint of blue, which gave Jen the hope of spring, and new beginnings.

* * * * *

"Hey, Chica, I'm home," Claire called as she closed the door behind her.

Jen stopped editing the photograph she was working on and looked up.

"Hi. How was your day?"

"Typical. You about finished?" Claire gestured toward the wedding photo displayed on the screen.

"Just about." Jen returned to her work, and added finishing touches to the picture.

"Great. I'm gonna get changed so we can start our cupcakes."

Each Monday night, the friends had a tradition of baking and decorating elaborate new cupcakes. This evening, they had in mind a decadent, dark chocolate

10

cake with chocolate espresso mousse filling.

Satisfied with her work, Jen shut down her computer. Claire was already in the kitchen getting things ready. After giving Jen an apron, she pulled ingredients out of the cupboards and refrigerator.

"So tell me about your date," Jen began. "What was his name, and where did you meet him?"

"Well," Claire placed a large bowl on the counter, "we met at the bank last week. His name is Ed, and boy was he a dud."

"What happened?"

"At first he seemed great." Claire sifted flour and baking soda together with some cocoa. "He was cute, and really funny when I talked to him at the bank, with the perfect amount of flirtiness."

"I didn't know there was a perfect amount of flirtiness." Jen laughed as she beat eggs and milk in a bowl.

"Oh, there definitely is. It's just enough so that you know he's interested, but not so much you think he can't talk to a woman without hitting on her. Anyway, when he met me downstairs, I made a joke—something about how I hoped the paycheck he was depositing would be enough to cover our date that morning. To which he replied, 'Paycheck? Oh, I don't have a job. I was at the bank paying some overdraft fees.'"

"Yikes." Jen winced. "Well, that's happened to all

of us at one time or another, right?"

Jen took the bowl of dry ingredients Claire handed her, and then added the egg mixture. Slowly her friend beat them all together with a whisk.

"Right, that's why I dropped the subject. I figured he was just between jobs, or going to school, or something. So, then he tells me that we're going to walk to Buddie's Diner for breakfast. We get there and order. I had some egg combo thing and a cup of coffee. He asked for this hungry man platter with a tall stack of pancakes as a side dish, juice, *and* a Grande Frappuccino."

"Wow. That's quite an appetite." Jen turned on the oven to pre-heat it.

"My thoughts exactly." Claire beat the batter more violently with each sentence. "So, as we're talking, I find out that not only does he *not* have a job, but he has no intention of getting one. Instead, he's in the process of figuring out a way to beat the system, and live off the government."

"Gee, he sounds like a real prize."

"It gets better. We finished our meal, and the bill came. He looked at me and says, 'Hey Babe, could you get this one? I still owe my buddy some cash for those overdrafts.' Can you believe that? As if we've gone out dozens of times with his money, and now I owe him."

Jen placed paper cupcake liners into two pans,

and then used a large ice cream scoop to fill each one with equal amounts of batter.

"So did you pay the bill?"

"Sort of."

Jen paused, batter dripping from her scoop into the bowl, and looked at her friend. "Umm, Claire. How can you *sort of* pay a bill?"

"Well, that's the best part. Just as the waitress brought it, he got up and went to the bathroom. I asked her to split it. I paid for my part, plus a tip for the whole portion, since I figured he'd probably be too cheap to give her anything decent. Then, I left. Ha ha. That'll teach him."

"No, you didn't." Jen's jaw dropped.

"I sure did."

"Claire, you amaze me." She put the trays into the hot oven. "I wish I had your guts."

"Trust me, start going on as many dates as I do, and things like that won't even faze you. You've got to weed out the bad ones to get to the worthwhile guys."

The heavenly scent of rich chocolate and roasted coffee beans filled the kitchen. Claire made a cup of espresso, and Jen melted chocolate chips in a double boiler for their mousse filling.

"Speaking of dating," Claire added, "were there any hotties at the wedding on Saturday?"

"Of course. There are always good looking guests.

You know how it goes—even if I would accept a date from someone I met there, it's hard for me to get serious when I work during the weekdays *and* every weekend."

"You see, that's your problem. You're looking for something serious, like a boyfriend, or a relationship."

"What's wrong with that?" Jen combined her chocolate with Claire's espresso and whipped them together.

"Nothing's wrong with it, it's just got to be dull for you. I mean, I know I'm great to hang out with and all," Claire joked, "but it's nice to get taken out every once in a while."

"I'll give you that." Jen sighed, lifting and dropping her shoulders.

"Keep yourself open to new dating possibilities. In the meantime, I'll find someone for you to go out with."

"Uh, you mean like a blind date?" She took a step back.

"Yes, exactly like a blind date. It will give you a chance to get back into the dating scene. This way, if the guy turns out to be a total bum, you don't ever have to see him again. Okay?"

As Jen finished whipping the mousse filling, she considered Claire's proposition. Despite her reluctance, excitement stirred inside her at the thought of meeting someone new. "Yeah. Okay." She set down the whisk and nodded resolutely.

The oven timer sounded. Claire pulled open the door and sweetly scented warm air flooded the tiny space.

Once the girls placed the cupcakes on a cooling rack, they put a large, frozen, pepperoni pizza on the pizza stone and placed it in the oven.

"So tell me..." Claire smirked. "Was that gorgeous blonde bartender, Matty, working this weekend? He's always flirting with you. Oh, you should date him. Can you imagine the kids you two would have?"

Once Matty had given Jen a ride home when her car was in the shop. Since meeting him, Claire had yet to forget his uncommon good looks.

"Whoa. Let's not get ahead of ourselves here. Anyway, I thought you wanted me to date casually."

"Right. I do. I'm just kidding. So tell me, was he working?"

The girls made their way to the couch. Each wrapped a worn knit blanket around her shoulders.

"No. He was off. There was a new guy, though. He's Al's nephew, his name's Nate. He'll be doing DJ work while Al and his wife go on their trip."

"Tell me about him." She patted the couch cushion in her excitement.

"He seems like he'll do a pretty good job. Al mentioned that he worked for him before. He seemed confident—at least the little I saw of him."

"No. I don't mean tell me what he's like as a DJ. I mean, tell me *about* him. What does he look like? Is he hot?"

Jen shrugged. "He's average, I guess."

"Average?" She frowned. "Average? What does that even mean?"

"I mean, he's just normal. Average height, dark brown hair, typical face, probably about our age, twenty-four or twenty-five." Jen thought for a moment. "I guess he did have nice teeth."

"Oh my goodness. I ask you to tell me about a guy, and all you can say is he has nice teeth." Claire tossed a pillow at her. "Artist types are all the same. You notice the weirdest stuff. I'm surprised you didn't tell me he has great elbows, or something like that."

"Well, I couldn't get a look at his elbows while he's wearing a tux, now could I?" Jen giggled. "I'll have to keep you posted on the elbow front."

"Yes, please do," Claire said, in mock seriousness. "I think our cupcakes are cool enough. Do you wanna fill them now?"

"Mmm hmm!" She licked her lips.

The girls got up and made their way back to the kitchen.

"Oh, this is definitely one for the wall," Claire declared, when they had finished piping the espresso mousse into each cake and topped them with an extra swirl of the richly flavored filling.

Jen dusted their creations artfully with chocolate sprinkles. Then, she stepped back to join Claire as she admired their work. "I'll get my camera."

Within a few moments, she had put on her macro lens, and the mini dye-sub printer started up. Placing one cake on a white square plate, she snapped a couple of photos.

Jen plugged her camera into the little printer. "This might be one of my favorites."

Seconds later, an image of their mini masterpiece emerged.

"Perfect." Claire took the picture and examined it closely.

By this time, their pizza was ready and the oven timer sounded.

"Food's done." Claire gave the photo back to Jen, and then put on her oven mitts to remove their dinner.

Jen walked to the bulletin board that hung on the kitchen wall. The corkboard that was once home to phone numbers and weekly reminders was now covered with pictures. Their baked goods were worthy works of art.

"Mmmm. I'm starving." Jen pinned the photograph with the others, and then turned to face Claire.

"Me, too." Claire picked a crisp piece of pepperoni from the pie, and popped it into her mouth. "Our show's about to start. You know, if this blind date thing doesn't work out, we could always sign you up for one of these dating shows."

Jen laughed. "It's good to know you have such confidence in the guy you're going to choose for me."

With that, the women carried their dinner, bubbling colas, and a tray of their latest creations to the couch, where they each sank in to enjoy an evening of good food, good company, and reality dating shows.

CHAPTER THREE

Freshly brewed morning coffee in hand, Jen sat on a kitchen stool, flipping absentmindedly through a magazine.

"Mornin' Doll," Claire greeted as she entered the kitchen, rubbing sleep from her eyes. "I can't believe you're still in your pajamas this late on a Saturday."

The week had passed like any other. Days evaporated at the computer, while Jen color corrected, cropped, then ordered proofs. Finally, she prepared for the next wedding, and the process would start all over again.

"I know. I can't say I object. The wedding I'm shooting today is kind of old fashioned, if you ask me. No getting-ready pictures, no fun bridal party stuff — just the ceremony and formal family shots. I was explicitly instructed not to take candid or party pictures at the reception — only a few for each big moment."

"Wow. So by old fashioned, you mean totally boring." Claire gave an exaggerated thumbs-down.

"Call it what you will. But, if it means I get to

sleep an extra couple of hours on a Saturday, that's fine with me. Not to mention, if all weddings were exactly the same, that would get pretty dull."

Claire joked, "And with the weddings being so different, it gives you a wider range of men to choose from."

"You're unbelievable." Jen got up from her seat and poked her friend with her elbow before heading back to her bedroom. "I'm gonna get dressed."

Jen stood in front of her closet, deciding which outfit would best match the style of that day's wedding. In her day-to-day life, she enjoyed expressing her artistic energy by layering clothes and accessories with different colors or patterns, or by wearing bright, colorful things. On Saturdays, while working, she preferred to go simple. She liked to imagine herself as a shadow, moving silently along the walls of the church, unnoticed by the guests, and certainly not seen by the bride or groom.

After a minute of mind designing, she pulled a knee length, charcoal-gray wrap dress out of the closet. She then added black tights and black wedge heels. *Perfect. Now for hair and makeup.* Spending several minutes in front of the bathroom mirror, she perfected the pinning of her hair into a chignon at the nape of her neck. Then, after giving her cheeks and lips a hint of color, she added a smoky gray shadow to her eyes.

Satisfied with her final look, Jen made her way back into the living room. "Well, I'm heading out now," she called to her roommate.

"You want me to help you carry your things downstairs?" Claire looked up from her spot on the couch.

"That'd be great. Thanks." Jen pulled on her high necked, wool coat.

The girls gathered up Jen's equipment bags, purse, and reusable grocery bag filled with food and drinks for the day. Together they descended the six flights of stairs to the cold outdoors.

After placing her things in the trunk, Jen closed it up, as Claire made her way back towards the apartment.

"Have a good day," Jen called to her friend who was standing in the building doorway.

"You, too!"

* * * * *

Jen arrived at the church thirty minutes before the wedding party, giving herself ample time to review what had been gone over at the rehearsal.

Let's see – the groom enters through these doors. So, if I'm standing here, I can get his picture, and then have plenty of time to move those few feet over to there, before the bridesmaids take their walk down the aisle.

With the entire ceremony running through her mind, Jen mapped out the quickest route to capture the best images. In her last free moments, she took pictures of the front of the church and the altar, where the couple would stand.

Guests were arriving and seating themselves when the groom's limo pulled up. Waiting in the doorway to usher the men in, Jen, seeing the morose expressions on their faces, half expected to see a hearse pulling up behind them.

The groom, a short, middle-aged man with graying hair, offered his hand to Jen. "Hello, Miss Schuman. We're pleased you're here."

"Well, thank you." Although she'd had several conversations with the groom prior to the wedding, she was, each time, taken aback by his unchanging and serious nature. "The church looks wonderful. I hope it's a lovely day for you."

After a slight pause, looking completely indifferent, he stated, "I'm sure everything will be satisfactory. I'll see you after the ceremony. Good day." With that, he and his stoic groomsmen walked away.

* * * * *

The ceremony was flawless, but somber. First, a sullen bride, wearing a semi-cathedral length veil, made her way down the aisle in an ivory gown. After two lifeless readings, the Reverend gave his address. Next, the bride and groom exchanged traditional vows and rings. The tight-lipped peck that concluded the ceremony seemed more like a seal of agreement than a romantic gesture. During the entire event, Jen felt as if she were documenting some sort of business transaction, rather than capturing the start of two lives together. *To each his own, I guess.*

* * * * *

When the family had gathered after the ceremony Jen addressed the group. "All right everyone, if you could please have a seat in the front pews, I'll call you as needed for the formal pictures. That will make this as quick and painless as possible." While the bridal party and family did obey her instructions, their lack of smiles showed Jen her attempt at a joke wasn't well received.

The silence among the group set her on edge.

"Could I please have our lovely bride?" She waited patiently until the bride arrived. "If you'll stand on this top step, I'll adjust your train." Jen took hold of the of the bride's gown. With a quick flourish, she draped it beautifully down the three lower steps. "Gorgeous. Now, if you could please turn just a little to the side—lovely, just like that. Hold your flowers near your hip, and with both hands. Excellent. On three. One. Two. Three." The bride gave a tight-lipped smile, and Jen pressed the shutter button.

After a few similar shots from varying angles, Jen requested the groom.

"Sir, if you'd please stand by your new wife. Yes,

right there. Put your arm around her waist, and your opposite hand on hers…just like that."

The groom did as asked, and the pictures continued as before. Though the ever-obedient group posed exactly as instructed, in no way did they acknowledge that they were participating in an exciting, enjoyable, experience. *Bride and groom together, check.* Jen made mental notes as she went about her work. *Couple with each set of their parents, check. Bride and groom with the best man and maid of honor, check. Entire bridal party, and I'm done.*

"We're all finished," Jen addressed the bride and groom, "unless you have anything else you'd like me to photograph."

The groom looked blankly at her. "No, I think we're fine. Thank you very much."

"Thank you. I'll see you at the Ivy Manor, then."

"Very good." The groom joined his family and the bridal party as they exited the church.

Whew. Jen breathed a sigh of relief, as she watched the group leave, then took a seat on one of the pews. *Boy, I'm glad they didn't want formal pictures with their extended families.*

While more boisterous bridal parties often became difficult to organize, they at least added to the joy that Jen found in taking pictures. If possible, this group sucked it out of her.

After taking a moment to collect herself, Jen

packed up her things and headed to the car. Traveling the familiar streets to the Ivy Manor, she searched her bag for a granola and snacked on it as she drove.

Pulling her sedan into one of the spaces furthest from the door, Jen turned off her car, gathered her equipment, and made her way toward the huge, white, ivy-covered building.

The Manor, originally a nineteenth century mansion, was home to three different reception locations. The first was the outdoor garden area, which, until the spring arrived, wouldn't be used. The second was a cozy mid-sized hall, its two large fireplaces on either side of the room being the draw for many couples who were looking to have an intimate winter wedding. The last hall, called the grand ballroom, was the location for that evening's reception. It boasted high ceilings, tall windows, French doors that led to the gardens, and crystal chandeliers that offered soft twinkling lights that danced along the pale hardwood floor.

Climbing the stairs and making her way between the ivy covered columns, Jen pulled the heavy door open and entered the foyer. Taking a look around, she searched for Al or Frankie to let them know she'd arrived.

The entrance to the manor was much like the grand ballroom, with the same hardwood floors throughout. Here, though, an elaborate Persian-style rug partially covered the area, while another larger, more ornate crystal chandelier hung from the cathedral ceiling.

The foyer had an immense staircase that swirled upward along the wall. These steps led to the upstairs office and meeting rooms, where soon-to-be brides and grooms planned the details of their receptions.

After placing her equipment behind the DJ stand, Jen walked into the kitchen, where she found the brothers reviewing the details for the night with the assistant chefs, bartenders, and serving staff.

"All right everyone, remember," Frankie instructed, "this is a no-nonsense affair. We need quick and quiet service, all night. Unless anyone has questions, you're free to finish prepping your areas for the evening. Thanks, everyone."

The members of the small crowd dispersed, and returned to their previous tasks.

"Afternoon, gentlemen, and I use the term loosely," Jen joked.

"There's our girl," Frankie boomed.

"How'd the ceremony go?" Al patted her on the shoulder.

"Dull, and unnervingly quiet at times. But otherwise fine." She laughed aloud. "Do you have a schedule of the evening's events?"

"Sure do," Al answered, pointing to the adjacent room. "It's on top of the mixer in the ballroom."

"Thanks. I'm gonna give it a look, so I'll know what's happening tonight. I'll see you in there."

The click of Jen's heels against the hardwood floor echoed off the walls as she walked through the ballroom. Weaving her way through the tables, she admired the crisp ivory linens that covered them, as well as the matching chair covers. Paired with table linens were black napkins, expertly crown folded and set on top of each guest's place setting. Low vases filled with deep red roses pulled the entire look together.

Jen located the schedule and reviewed it.

"Can I help you with something?"

The voice made her jump. Looking to her right she saw Al's dark haired nephew slipping from behind a large speaker, connection wires in hand.

"Oh, I'm sorry. Nate, I'm Jen, the photographer. We met last week," Jen sputtered, sticking out her hand.

"I know. I'm just giving you a hard time." Chuckling, he quickly dropped what he was holding and took her hand. "Good to see you again."

His laugh showed his straight, white teeth, and it made Jen think of her deal with Claire to check out his elbows, which were currently covered by a white dress shirt.

"You, too," Jen agreed.

"So, are you all ready for this evening?"

"I don't actually have too much to do." She shrugged. "It was made very clear to me that I'm not to be portraying this as a big party. I'm allowed to take pictures of the important moments and nothing else." She moved her arms in a rigid fashion to further show the strictness of her instructions.

"Yeah, we got the same orders. Our playlist tonight will be limited to classical piano pieces and the occasional light jazz instrumental," he said in a voice imitating a waiter at a fancy restaurant informing a patron of an evening's specials.

Jen laughed. "Well, at least we'll all be bored to tears together." She looked down at the schedule in her hand. "So what have we got here?"

Nate moved behind her and read over her shoulder. "Well, first is cocktail hour, then the couple will arrive, next the Reverend will say grace and dinner will be served. After they eat, the bride and groom cut the cake, and that's it. No first dance together or anything."

"Sounds easy enough."

"Sure does. Well, I better get back to setting up. Guests will be here in the next hour or so."

"I'm gonna get myself organized, too." She put down the paper. "Let me know if you need any help. I've got a lot less to prepare than you do."

"Thanks, I will."

As if on cue, almost exactly an hour later, guests

wandered in, taking in the elegant ballroom as they were offered hors d'oeuvres and glasses of champagne. Piano concertos poured from the speakers and mingled with the quiet murmur of conversations amongst the guests.

"Looks like they're here," Nate said as he glanced out the window to where the couple's limo had pulled up to the door. "Al is nowhere in sight. Guess I'm on my own, huh?" He took a deep breath.

"You'll do fine." Jen reassured him with a smile before heading towards the door.

"Here goes nothing."

Nate faded out the classical piece as the bride and groom entered the foyer.

"Ladies and gentlemen," his smooth, strong voice spoke over the music, "it's my honor to welcome Mr. and Mrs. Albert Wagner."

Three hundred guests politely applauded as Albert and his wife, Rita, entered the reception hall. While arm in arm, gently waving at their friends and family, they looked at everyone but each other. As soon as they had walked the length of the ballroom, the pair took their seats at the head table and waited for the Reverend to offer grace.

Feeling as if prayer wasn't something the couple would appreciate having photographed, Jen followed suit and took her seat at the staff table.

"Sorry about that, Nate." Jen overheard Al's

usually booming voice whisper when the prayer ended. "Frankie was a bit understaffed in the kitchen, so I got caught up in prepping salads. Did everything go all right?"

"It seemed to. Nobody got up and left." Nate joked.

As the meal was served, things at the bar slowed, and Jen could see Matty standing behind it. His intentionally disheveled, blonde hair and intense green eyes, along with his strong build that was apparent even through his dress clothes, made him incredibly appealing to look at. The way he carried himself gave an air of cockiness, but women easily and often overlooked that when he started his smooth talking. Making eye contact with Jen, he signaled for her to come over with a jerk of his head.

He is good looking, Jen admitted to herself, remembering her best friend's earlier comments, and trying to keep the sly smile from showing on her face.

"Hey, Babe. You're looking amazing as usual." Matty looked her up and down as she approached the bar. "Can I mix you a drink?"

And then he opens his mouth. She rolled her eyes at his usual inability to speak to a woman without coming on to her.

"Just my usual."

"Cranberry juice and a wedge of lime. You need to live a little." He filled her glass, grabbed a slice of lime from a bowl, and tossed it around his back, over his shoulder and into his opposite hand, showing off, before placing the wedge on the edge of her drink.

"Not while I'm working, I don't."

He let his fingers linger on hers as he handed her the beverage. Then, taking a shot glass from beneath the bar, poured himself a drink, took a quick look around to make sure no one was watching and whispered, "Bottoms up".

"You better watch it." Jen leaned toward him. "This is a pretty uptight group we've got tonight. I'm not sitting around here to watch you get yourself in trouble." She turned to make her way back to the staff table.

"Oh, you're no fun," Matty teased, as he swiftly whipped his arm out and tried to tap her with a towel.

"Thanks for the drink." She lifted it in appreciation.

Jen rejoined Al and Nate at their small table. Salads were already waiting at each person's place setting when she arrived, so they quickly passed around the rolls and butter to begin eating.

"Thanks, Angie," Jen said to a familiar server, who served them a bowl of rigatoni and meat sauce. "Al, you did a good job on these salads." She took an appreciative bite.

"Yeah, Uncle Al, it's good to know that when

you're no longer a good DJ, you have a career in cutting up lettuce to fall back on." Nate poked fun, jabbing a fork in his uncle's direction.

"For your information, smart aleck, this is spinach and arugula, not lettuce."

"Oh, well forgive me, Uncle. I forgot I was speaking with a professional." Nate chuckled. "I stand corrected."

As dinner progressed, Angie brought dish after dish for them to enjoy. Jen listened as Al talked about all the gossip Carol had shared with him that week, and as he and Nate discussed details of the upcoming weddings Nate would be handling for him.

"Looks like the bride and groom are just about finished eating. They'll be ready to cut their cake soon." Al gave Jen a heads up.

"Better get my camera ready."

The cake, like all other elements of the wedding, was very fine, but lacked any kind of personality. The only decoration on the round, tiered confection was a black ribbon of fondant that wrapped around the base of each layer.

"And now, friends and family," Jen heard Al's much subdued voice begin, "Albert and Rita will be cutting their wedding cake."

With that, they picked up a knife, removed a slice, and, using forks, fed each other a bite. After the usual applause, Jen waited, poised and ready to capture her favorite moment. She then realized the couple had used forks. The bride, while still chewing, simply handed the plate of half-eaten cake to a nearby server and walked away from her groom. Disappointed, Jen slowly lowered her camera and watched as an unfazed groom did the same.

"You all right?" Jen heard when she reached the staff table again.

"What? Oh, yeah, just thinking," she answered automatically, surprised to see Nate looking at her with a curious expression on his face.

"'Bout what?"

"I don't know." Jen dropped her voice to a whisper and looked around to make sure no one was listening. "Do you ever kind of feel bad for the bride and groom?" She placed the lens cap back on her camera.

"How so?"

"Well, you're going to think I'm crazy," Jen continued quietly, "but you know when the couple cuts the cake?"

"Yeah."

"Well, right after that, when they're done feeding each other, I love to watch what they do with the frosting that's left over on their fingers."

"Okay." Nate raised an eyebrow.

"You think I'm kinda weird, don't you?" She removed the flash from her camera and packed the equipment into her bag.

"No, I'm just wondering why that makes you feel bad for the bride and groom."

"Oh, well I don't feel bad for all of them." Jen laughed. She sat on the edge of the DJ stand. "Just today. You see, some couples are so sweet. They goof around, and clean each other up, stuff like that. But today," Jen's voice grew softer, "I don't know, seeing the two of them walk away from each other, not caring. I felt like it showed me a little too much of what their life is going to be like together. Does that make sense?"

"Sure it does. I used to look at that kind of stuff, too." He sat down on the podium beside her. "I mean, all right, don't think I'm awful, but a guy can only listen to those mushy father daughter songs so many times before he loses his mind, right?"

"That's understandable," Jen replied, amused.

"Well, after playing the same ones at almost every wedding, whenever the father of the bride danced with his daughter, I would watch the groom. Most guys take the opportunity to grab a drink at the bar, or talk to their friends, but once in a while, I'd see a guy who would watch his wife. I always figured those were the guys who were truly crazy about their wives, and were glad to be married."

"Wow, that might be better than my frosting theory." Jen nodded her head.

"Ha ha. Well, I don't know about that, but a guy's gotta do something to keep himself entertained while playing the same songs week after week. What about you, though? You must never get bored, since you get to see all the interesting stuff, being the photographer."

"Oh, there are definitely some characters."

"Tell me. Like who?" He waited with anticipation on his face.

"Let's see, I'd say, hands down the hardest people to deal with at any wedding are the aunts of the bride."

"Seriously?"

"Yep. I think it's because they're usually close enough to her that they feel special, but distant enough that they don't have to worry about the details that the paying parents do. Plus, that gives them more time to come up with photo ideas and tell me what pictures they feel I should be taking."

"Wow," he leaned back on his hands, thinking. "I can't believe people other than the bride and groom would have the nerve to do that."

"You'd be surprised." She chuckled. "So, tell me some inside DJ information. Who's the hardest for you to work with?"

"For me it's the bride and groom combo. I think for many men, the music is one of the few things they want to decide on for their wedding. Flowers, clothes, most of them don't care about that stuff. So when the couple comes in to meet with me, he knows his favorite songs and what he wants played, but then his fiancé will pull out a list she printed off the internet of romantic wedding songs. Then the battle begins."

"Well, I certainly do not envy you those meetings." They both laughed together. "I guess you have the same problem I do, then."

"What's that?" He leaned forward again, resting his arms on his knees.

"Just that we spend enough time with a couple that we get to see how they interact, and what they're really like, but not so much time that we ever figure out why they do what they do."

"That's it exactly!"

Al interrupted, "Hey, Nate, you planning on helpin' me out anymore tonight?"

"Guess I better get back to work." Nate stood up.

"Yeah, since there aren't any more big moments, and that's all the bride and groom wanted pictures of, I'm going to check in with them to see if they need anything else from me. If not, I get to head home early."

"Have a good night then, Kid-o." Al waved.

"Thanks. You guys, too. Night. It was nice talking to you, Nate."

"You, too. See ya next weekend."

* * * * *

That evening Jen pulled into her regular space at a record-breaking 7:00 p.m. With more energy than ever after a wedding, she gathered her things, hopped through the slush in the parking lot, and, as always, skipped the elevator, and walked the six flights of stairs to her apartment.

It was dark and still when she walked in. *It's early. Claire must still be out on a date.* Dropping her things by the door, she strolled to the blinking answering machine.

"Hi, Jen." An unfamiliar voice on the machine commenced after she pushed the play button. "My name is Steve. I work with your friend Claire. She gave me your number, and thought we should go out sometime. If you're interested, give me a call back. My number is 555-1426."

Well, that was quick. Jen looked at the clock. *Just a little after seven. I might as well call him now.*

Picking up the phone, she dialed his number. Her heart beat nervously as she waited.

"Hello." A voice answered after two rings.

"Hi. My name is Jen. May I please speak to Steve?"

"This is he. Hi. Thanks for calling me back. So, Claire mentioned weekends aren't good for you," he jumped in right away. "Would you be interested in going out to dinner with me one day this week?"

"Sure. That would be nice. Would Wednesday

work for you?" She tried to keep her voice light.

"Yes. Wednesday is perfect. Is there anything you do or don't like to eat?"

"Well, I'm allergic to most kinds of fish, but other than that I am pretty adventurous."

"Great. I'll keep that in mind. If I pick you up at seven does that sound good?"

"Seven sounds excellent. Do you know where I live?"

"With Claire, right? I have her address."

"Great. I'll see you Wednesday, then."

"Yes, see you then, Jen. Bye."

"Thanks. Bye."

Jen let out a deep sigh as she hung up the phone. *Well, today certainly turned out better than expected,* she thought, as she removed the bobby pins that held her hair in place and made her way down the hall. *First, I get home early, then I get a date. Maybe a bath will be the next step in the evening.* Jen turned on the hottest water in the tub that she could stand and poured some bubble bath under the stream. Dropping her bobby pins in a glass dish on the counter, she headed to the living room. She took a few candles from the coffee table and the latest magazines from the couch and placed them on the edge of the tub. After throwing her clothes in the wash, she returned to the tub and sank down into the hot water, surrounding herself with bubbles. *Not too bad at all, for a Saturday night.*

CHAPTER FOUR

"Jen, I'm home!" Claire called the following Wednesday afternoon. "Where are you?"

"In my room."

Claire appeared in Jen's doorway and moved to plop down on the corner of the bed, dropping her purse on the floor next to her. "Hey."

"Hey. How was your day? Why are you here so early?"

"I wanted to see you before your date."

"Well, I'm glad you're here, because I don't know what to wear. What's Steve like?" Jen rifled through her closet.

"Actually—to be honest—I don't know Steve all that well."

"What?" Stopping her search abruptly, Jen turned around.

"I mean..." Claire held her hands up in mock defense. "I know that he's single, and he seems nice enough. On the rare occasion that we run into each other at the office, he always says hello. It's just, I didn't want you to feel pressured to keep dating someone because they were a close friend of mine, so even though I don't know him very well, I picked Steve. This way, if you don't like him it's no biggie."

"Ugh. Well, when you put it that way I guess it makes sense." Jen plunked down on the mattress beside her friend, and shook her head giggling.

"Whew. I'm glad you see it the way I do." Claire looked relieved. "Now let's pick out something for you to wear."

* * * * *

Thirty minutes later Jen emerged from the bathroom. "How do I look?"

She wore a belted, cream colored, cowl neck sweater dress that fell to the middle of her thighs, with a pair of brown boots. Her blonde hair hung in loose waves, framing her face.

"Perfect. Sweetie, he'd be crazy not to fall instantly in love with you."

"Thanks. You're the best." She hugged her friend. "I better go. I've got an appointment with a customer at the Ivy Manor first. I don't want to be late. Will you be here when I get back, before Steve comes?"

"No, I have a date picking me up at six, so I'll see you when we both get home tonight."

"All right, have a good time."

"You, too. Good luck!"

* * * * *

Jen arrived at the Manor just moments before

five. She used her key to unlock the enormous front door and let herself in. Racing upstairs to her personal meeting room, she turned on the lights and gathered her sample books, a wedding questionnaire, and a contract. Just as she was making her way back down the swirling staircase to the foyer, the prodigious door opened, and in came the engaged couple.

"Hi. Welcome to the Ivy Manor. I'm Jen." She offered her hand as she reached the bottom of the stairs.

"Hi. I'm Emma, and this is my fiancé Aaron."

"Nice to meet you."

The young couple shook hands with Jen, and she ushered them upstairs to the prepared meeting room.

"Have a seat."

Aaron pulled out a chair for his soon-to-be bride, and took the one next to hers.

"All right, let's talk about your big day. Tell me first, what's your date?" Jen picked up a pen.

"It's the third Saturday in July. The twenty second," Emma answered. Aaron held her hand, and they looked into each other's eyes with a sweet, dreamy look.

"Okay." Jen jotted the date down on the questionnaire. "And have you spoken yet with Al or Frankie regarding which part of the Ivy Manor you'll be using for the reception?"

"Yes, but actually we'll be having both the

ceremony and reception on the beach. The Ivy Manor is catering and providing the music there," Emma clarified.

"That sounds nice. What time will it start?"

"We want the ceremony to end right about when the sun sets," Aaron said. "We're thinking around 7:30 or 8:00 p.m. Can we let you know when it gets closer to the time?"

"Absolutely. Now, tell me about your bridal party."

"Well, my sister is my maid of honor, and his little sister will be a junior bridesmaid."

"My best friend is my best man," Aaron continued. "The whole thing is going to be pretty small, so we aren't having any other bridesmaids or groomsmen."

"Great." Jen continued filling in the questionnaire. "And what about flower girls or ring bearers? Are you having either of those?"

"No," Emma replied.

"Easy enough," Jen continued. "Now, how about your ceremony? Other than the vows and exchanging rings, what other elements will be part of it?"

"We haven't spoken with the Justice of the Peace yet, but we'd like to include a poem, read by a close, mutual friend, and two of Aaron's cousins will be playing acoustic guitar instead of traditional walking down the aisle music."

"That sounds amazing." Jen pronounced with genuine ardor, as she pictured the evening in her mind. "Now for the reception, will you be having a cake cutting, first dance together, garter and bouquet toss, money dance?"

"We'll be cutting the cake, and we'd like to have a first dance, but we were thinking our best man and maid of honor would join us half way through instead of doing a separate bridal party dance. Can we do that?" Aaron wondered aloud.

"Absolutely. You can do anything you'd like. The Ivy Manor's DJ's are very flexible."

"Great. Oh, and Emma, you wanted to throw your bouquet, right?"

"Yes, definitely." She bounced excitedly in her chair.

Aaron put his arm around her and grinned.

"You two are adorable," Jen said aloud.

"Thanks." Emma giggled.

"All right, just a few more questions and we'll be finished. Do you want getting ready pictures, and, if so, when and where would you like those to take place?" Jen looked to Emma.

"Yes, that'd be great. I'll be getting ready at my parents' house around four."

"Good, and as far as bridal party and formal family pictures go, usually the bridal party will go to a separate location for pictures after taking formal family shots at the ceremony site. Since yours will all be in the same spot, what would you like to do?"

"Well, our siblings are all in the bridal party, so that just leaves our parents to do formal pictures with," Aaron said. "We were thinking we'd like to do all of our pictures right down the beach from where everyone else will be having the cocktail hour. Will that work?"

"I don't see why not. Okay, last question for today," Jen put down her pen and, placing her elbows on the table, pressed her finger tips together. "Can you give me a few words describing the overall feel you want your wedding to have?"

"That's a hard one." Emma looked at Aaron for ideas. After a moment she spoke. "Warm, like in the summer when it's sunny and everyone seems content and happy. That's what I want our wedding to be like."

"Sounds perfect." Aaron leaned in and gave her a kiss on the cheek.

"Well, I have to say, your wedding seems like a photographer's dream come true," Jen exclaimed, feeling inspired. "We'll be meeting again in the next couple of months. In the meantime, it's good to keep a list of any additional people or details that are important to you. That way I can use the list to make sure I get pictures of all of those things. Okay?"

"Sure, we can do that." Emma nodded.

Jen led them back to the foyer and bade them a good evening after having gone over the details of the contract with them and collecting the couple's deposit check.

Still caught up in the glow of her meeting, she let herself get lost in thought as she drove home to meet her date. *What an amazing couple. The way they really seem to be planning this together and truly care what the other person thinks is so unusual. Every detail of their wedding is so personal, so thought out, and so them. It's just perfect. To have that would be so nice.* Jen pulled into the driveway for her apartment building and parked her car. *How great would it be to have a relationship like Emma and Aaron's? To meet someone, and grow close and comfortable. A man I could talk to about day-to-day things and build interests with. So much like a best friend. Perhaps today will be the day for it.*

Walking up the stairs, Jen knew her date with Steve was intended to be a way to start dating for fun, but she couldn't help dream that maybe he would be the person she'd been missing. For the first time in a while, Jen felt hope, excitement, and butterflies at the thought of the possibilities that lay ahead of her.

CHAPTER FIVE

$\mathbf{B}$ack in her apartment, Jen was nervous and alternated between pacing through the living room and sitting on the edge of the couch, bouncing her knees up and down. She repeatedly looked at the time. Never having been on a blind date, her usual fortitude and confidence wavered as she waited.

Five minutes 'til he's supposed to be here. Three minutes. Maybe I should go downstairs and wait there. Will that seem too desperate? No, just wait here 'til he rings the buzzer. Seven o'clock. I wonder where he is. 7:01 p.m. Well if I haven't heard from him by seven thirty, I'll assume he's not coming and I'll...

The sound of the apartment buzzer startled Jen out of her all-consuming nervous thoughts and made her jump up and dash to the speaker near the door. She took a deep breath.

"Hello."

"Hi. It's Steve."

"Hi, Steve. I'll be right down."

Jen grabbed her keys, put them in her purse, and, after shutting off the lights and locking the door behind her, descended the usual six flights of stairs.

"Hi, Steve. I'm Jen," she introduced herself as she neared the bottom step.

"Wow! Claire told me you were pretty, but wow!" He appeared delighted as he ardently looked her up and down.

"Oh, umm, thank you." Feeling uncomfortable she put a self-conscious hand to her hair, as he moved in and gave her a quick hug.

Although Jen hadn't had a clear picture in her mind of what she anticipated Steve looking like, he somehow wasn't what she expected. Standing about five-foot-eight, he was just a few inches taller than she would have been if she hadn't been wearing heels. In her current footwear he only had about an inch on her. His sandy brown hair was wavy and parted neatly on the side; his full face featured a prominent nose and a pair of wire rimmed glasses. The pastel colored dress shirt he wore was tucked into his black slacks. The word "tidy" came to Jen's mind.

"Should we head out?" Steve looked to the door.

"Yes, let's," Jen agreed kindly. "Where are we headed?"

"The Great Lakes Fish Market. It's my favorite place. Have you been there?"

"Uh, no. No, I haven't."

Jen considered her earlier phone conversation with Steve, and an array of thoughts ran through her mind. *I did tell him I was allergic to fish, right? Maybe he just didn't hear me, or maybe he forgot. Should I say something? I don't want him to feel bad. It was obviously just an accident. I'm sure there is something I can eat there. I'll just not mention it.*

"Well, the Lake Erie perch is excellent. You'll love this place."

Reaching Steve's black sports car, he unlocked the driver's side and got in without so much as a glance at Jen.

"Oh, sorry." He pressed the button on his door to unlock the passenger side for her.

"Thanks." She slid down into the leather bucket seat.

Steve started the car and started the drive down the busy street toward the restaurant. After a significant pause, Jen commenced their conversation.

"So, I know you work at the same company as Claire, but not in her department. What do you do?"

Steve cleared his throat. "I'm a managerial accountant."

"Oh, really. Have you been there long?" Jen looked in his direction as she waited for his reply.

"Well, I was originally a temp for the company, assisting one of the bookkeepers during the summer while I was in college. They knew I was getting my degree in accounting, so when I graduated, they offered me a position. It was just entry level, but since then I've worked my way up. I've got my master's now, and sometime in the next couple of years I hope to be head of the department."

As he spoke, Steve glanced from the road toward Jen, though she noticed that more often than not, he seemed to be studying her bare thigh rather than her face.

"Good for you. It sounds like you're quite motivated." She tried to sound more at ease than she was feeling.

"Yeah, it's good money, and you know how it goes. The higher you climb on the corporate ladder, the more there is to make."

"I guess so."

"So, Claire works in the lab, right?" He drummed his fingers against the steering wheel.

"Yes. She's a chemist. She's great at what she does. She's the youngest person in her department. Maybe even the youngest to ever work in that area."

"What's the deal with her hair?" Steve slowed the car and put on his turn signal as they approached the restaurant.

"What do you mean?"

"Like, why is it always different colors? She'd look better as a blonde, like you."

"Blonde isn't her style." Jen felt the need to defend her best friend. "She needs something more striking to express herself. I think the pink is awesome, actually."

"Here we are." He pulled into a parking spot. "This is gonna be great. Just wait."

Steve exited the car and headed straight for the door of the restaurant, opening it to let himself in, then holding it open behind him for Jen.

"Welcome to the Great Lakes Fish Market." A friendly girl in her late teens greeted them. "A table for two this evening?"

"Yes," Steve answered.

"Right this way." She took two menus from the holder on the side of the hostess stand, and led them into the dining area.

The establishment was busy for a Wednesday night. There was a vast array of patrons enjoying their dinners. Wooden booths ran along the walls of the room and were filled with middle aged couples. Several families occupied the larger tables in the center. Jen watched as a mom and dad tried to subdue two wriggling preschoolers. At another table, a set of parents were talking about their days at work, while their elementary school aged son amused himself by half eating, half playing with his basket of fish sticks. In a corner booth, a toddler played in a highchair as his parents did their best to coerce him into eating his dinner.

"Here you are." The hostess stopped in front of a small booth, next to a couple of senior citizens who were finishing up a dessert, and laid down Jen and

Steve's menus. "Enjoy your meal."

"Thank you. We will," Jen replied.

"Must be family night or something." Steve scrunched up his face. "I don't usually come here on Wednesdays."

"That banner says, 'Every Wednesday kids eat free'." Jen pointed across the room. "I like that. I think when families fill a restaurant it's a good sign that there's something for everyone. Plus, it's nice that places offer specials. It gives people a chance to go out when they otherwise might not have been able to, you know?"

"Never thought about it. So, what do you think you're going to get?"

"Oh, I don't know. I need to look over this menu. What they're having sure looks good." Jen pointed to the dessert the elderly couple next to them enjoyed. "Excuse me, what is that you're eating? It looks delicious."

"It's the super peanut butter and banana sundae," the gentleman answered.

"We come here every week for one, as a special treat," his wife added, nodding her wrinkled face. "You should order one to share with your young lady." She addressed Steve. "It's very romantic."

"Thanks. Maybe we will." Jen grinned at the pair.

"You just start conversations with complete strangers like that?" Steve leaned in and whispered.

Jen couldn't put her finger on what it was, but something in his tone gave her the impression he disapproved.

"Sure, why not? Just being friendly is all." She tried not to sound defensive.

"Hi. I'm Mike," a waiter in jeans and a blue polo shirt interrupted. "I'll be your server. Can I take your drink order?"

"I think we've decided what we want." Steve jumped in. "I'll have the perch platter, with mashed potatoes and a root beer."

"And for you?" Mike inquired of Jen.

Jen's eyes scanned the menu.

"I'll take an unsweetened iced tea and the small grilled chicken salad," she answered, deciding on the first non-seafood item she spotted, "and definitely one of those peanut butter, banana, ice cream things." She motioned toward the table next to them.

"Good choice. I'll bring your drinks right out." The server gathered their menus off the table.

"Thanks." Jen watched the waiter walk away and turned back to Steve. "So, tell me more about yourself. What do you like to do for fun?"

"Well, until recently I spent most of my time in school, but now that I've finished I've taken up skiing again, in the wintertime. Do you ski?"

"No, I've never tried. Maybe you could teach me sometime."

"Yeah, sure. There's not much to it. So, what about you? You're a photographer, right?"

"Yes. I love it. I like that I get to be around people for what is usually one of the best days of their lives. I don't think many professions are like that, you know?"

"I guess not."

"Here are your beverages." Mike returned and set their drinks on two cocktail napkins.

"Thanks," they both replied simultaneously.

I wonder what Steve's thinking. Is he having a good time?

Jen looked up from her drink and their eyes met. She got in a quick smile before Steve looked away and glanced around the room.

He seems somewhat disinterested. Maybe he's just nervous, though.

"I like the atmosphere of this place." Jen attempted to continue the conversation after a significant and uncomfortable lull.

"It's pretty low key. Sometimes I come here with a couple of guys after work. Looks like our food is coming."

Mike set their plates in front of them. "Is there anything else I can get you right now?"

Jen looked to Steve.

"We're fine," he replied, already picking up his silverware.

"Thank you," she called to the waiter's back as he turned to leave. Jen felt a sense of relief that there would be something to occupy their time now that their dinners had arrived. "This looks good. Let's dig in." Jen watched as Steve cut pieces of perch and dunked them deep into his dish of tartar sauce before taking a bite of her own food.

What else can I ask him about?

"So, what's your family like?" She inquired between bites.

"Pretty typical, I guess." He took a bite of mashed potatoes. "My parents are divorced."

"I'm sorry to hear that." Jen frowned.

"Well, that's pretty much the norm anymore, you know? I've got two older brothers that both live out of state."

"Are you close with them?"

"We see each other on holidays and send each other an email once a month or so, but they've both got families. We're all pretty caught up in our own lives." He dunked another large piece of perch.

"That's too bad."

"Ah, not really. You pick your friends, not your family, right?"

Jen didn't know how to respond. She always felt family was an important part of life.

I guess I don't know what it's like to have a family that isn't all that close. Maybe you just fill the space with great friendships. That's nice too, I'm sure. She tried to empathize.

Both of them were nearing the end of their meals, when Mike returned to their table with Jen's dessert, two spoons and the check.

"Wanna share?" She passed him the silverware.

"No thanks."

"All right. More for me, I guess," she joked uneasily.

Silence spread between them as she ate her dessert.

When Jen scraped the bottom of her sundae glass with the spoon, Steve looked at his watch impatiently.

"You about ready?"

"Yes. I'm stuffed. That couple was right. That sundae is definitely worth a weekly trip. Thank you very much for dinner," she acknowledged, as they made their way to the register.

"Sure."

* * * * *

Steve drove into the parking lot of Jen's apartment building and stopped in a spot near the door. Jen unbuckled her seat belt and hesitated to see what he would do. When he left the car running, she started talking again.

"Well, thank you again for dinner and the nice evening."

"Yeah. We should do it again sometime." He

leaned over and gave her a one armed hug. "See ya."

"Bye." Jen exited the car. "Drive safe." She closed the door behind her.

Steve backed out and was across the lot, waiting to pull onto the street, by the time Jen made it to the front door.

Letting herself in, she slowly climbed the steps.

Is there something wrong with me? She had a general feeling of disappointment regarding the evening as a whole. *I just went on my first date in ages, shouldn't I be happier?*

He was nice enough. I mean, it's not like he was flat out rude or anything. He wasn't unattractive. Sure, he didn't ask me much about myself, or respond to things that didn't have to do with him, but some people are just uneasy with those getting-to-know-you questions. He did say he wanted to do it again, so he couldn't have felt it was too bad.

By the time Jen reached her door, she was angry at herself for being bothered by the evening.

Feeling more exhausted than she had anticipated at only nine o'clock, she went to her room to change into a pair of sweats. Jen lay down on the couch, just wanting to flip through the channels so she wouldn't over-analyze every detail of the night as she was tempted to do. *That can wait till Claire comes home.* With that she began her channel surfing.

CHAPTER SIX

J en arrived early to the local community college where she and Claire took their Thursday night baking class together. Entering the empty classroom, she set her things down at their favorite baking station and removed her coat.

"Hey, Claire. Over here." Jen waved to her friend when she saw her in the doorway.

"Hi, Girlie. How was your day?" Claire made her way between ovens, counters, and other arriving classmates towards her friend. "Did you get my note this morning?"

"My day was nice, and, yeah, I did. Thanks."

"Oh, good. By the time I got home from my date last night, you were totally zonked on the couch, and I didn't want to wake you. When I was about to leave this morning, I saw you were still asleep, so I figured you probably needed the rest. That must have been some date. Do tell."

Their instructor stepped up to the front of the class, her voice interrupting their conversation. "All right, everyone, we're going to begin our section on batters made with fruit. Today it's just a simple banana nut cupcake with a honey, nut, and cream cheese frosting." She raised the recipe card held in her hand. "A copy of the recipe is at each of your stations. I'll be walking around, so let me know if you have questions."

Claire picked up the recipe, and they both looked it over. "You wanna mash up the bananas and do the wet ingredients, while I measure out the dry stuff?"

"Sounds good to me." Jen plucked three very ripe bananas off a bunch on a nearby counter and removed their darkening peels.

Claire collected the necessary tools from the cupboards below their station and the pantry area on the other side of the room, then sifted flour and baking soda into a medium-sized bowl.

"So tell me. I'm dying to know. How did everything go with Steve?"

"It was okay."

"Just okay? Bummer. I was hoping it was going to be amazing. I want to hear everything from the beginning."

Jen squashed the soft fruit in a large bowl and added softened butter.

"Well, as soon as I got downstairs, I introduced myself, and right off the bat he said how pretty I am. I mean, don't get me wrong, I want to feel I look good, but it was just the way he said it. That plus the fact that it was the first thing out of his mouth, without a hello or anything, I don't know, it made me kind of uncomfortable." She raised her shoulders, scrunching up her nose as she did.

"Uh, yeah." Claire rolled her eyes. "That's totally inappropriate. Some guys just don't get stuff like that. If they're going to comment on a girl's looks at the get-go, they need to be careful to be gentlemanly."

"Definitely. Like saying 'You look lovely' is absolutely appropriate."

"Sure, or commenting on a specific, but not too personal thing, like saying 'that's a cool necklace', or 'I like your hair like that'. Things of that nature."

"Totally." Jen laughed. "I'm glad I'm not the only one who thinks this stuff."

"You're not alone." She shook her head. "So go on, where did he take you?"

"The Great Lakes Fish Market."

"What?" Claire dropped her utensils with a loud clang into her bowl.

Jen lifted an apologetic hand to the room.

"You told him you were allergic to fish, right?"

"On the phone I did."

Claire placed a hand on her hip. "And he still took you there?"

"He said it was his favorite place."

"Oh, for crying out loud." Claire's volume increased. "That's ridiculous. I don't care if he *owned* the place. That was completely thoughtless."

The corners of Jen's mouth turned up as she tried to stifle a laugh at the fit of rage that was brewing in her best friend. It's not that she wanted Claire to be mad, but it made her feel good to see that she wasn't wrong in her thoughts that the evening could have gone better.

"So, do I even want to hear how the rest of this date went?" Claire asked, as the two friends combined the wet and dry ingredients together.

"Believe it or not, there isn't much more to tell. Our conversation was stiff—a *lot* of silence. I figured that was usual for a blind date. It seems to me, though, that the few topics we did cover, we have very different views on."

"Give me an example."

"Hmm, let's see." Jen stirred the mixture thoughtfully. "He made a couple of comments about making money. That's fine and all, it's just not my life's ambition, you know? And he doesn't seem like much of a family guy."

"So, how did you leave it?"

"Well, he gave me a one-armed hug in the car, while it was running, and said we should do it again."

"Wow. I'm sorry I set you up with such a jerk."

"Don't be. It was nice to get dressed up and go out."

The two worked in silence for a few moments as

they scooped batter into a dozen yellow paper cupcake liners.

"You know..." Jen pondered the evening in her mind. "I can't help but wonder if I went into the date all wrong."

"How so?"

"Well, remember the meeting I had before my date?"

"Yeah."

"That couple, they were so great. When I left the Manor, they had me thinking about what I want in a relationship. By the time Steve got there, I think I was back to my old ways. You know, looking for a relationship, not just a fun date. He probably won't call me, but if for some reason he did, I think I'd give him another chance."

"Seriously?" Claire was appalled.

"Yes, seriously. I mean, I know he isn't a guy I'd want to spend the rest of my life with, but compared to some of the horror stories you've told me, he didn't do anything outrageously wrong. Everyone deserves a second chance, right?"

"Wow. Well, you're a lot more understanding than I would be. Let me go on the record saying I am not crazy about you going out with him again. I get what you mean about going into dates with a different attitude, but you can do that with a new guy."

"Duly noted. I'm guessing he's not going to call anyhow, so it's kind of a moot point. Anyway, you can't be gloomy when making frosting, so let's talk about happier things. I want to hear all about your date last night."

"Actually, it was quite fun."

"That's great. What's the guy's name? Where did you meet this one?"

Jen beat a softened block of cream cheese in a metal bowl, as Claire measured some honey and added it to the mix.

"His name's Kyle. We met last week at Java Jane's. I had a taste for one of those salted hot chocolates, so I stopped by on my lunch hour. He was in line, too. We started talking about menu items, and it went from there."

"Awww. Tell me more. Where did he take you?"

"We went to that 50's diner. It was totally not where I expected to go on a first date, but I was pleasantly surprised by his creativity. It's a fun atmosphere, and who doesn't like that type of greasy spoon, comfort food?"

Claire opened the oven and removed the tray of cupcakes, allowing them to cool, as Jen finely ground some pecans in a food processor for the frosting.

"That's good. So, what did you talk about?"

"Hmm. Mostly getting-to-know-you things. He's an IT guy, so obviously he knows a lot about computers. We talked about the old days when he was so into them that he'd only tear himself away from the screen long enough to down some caffeine and microwave a pizza."

"Ha ha." Jen chuckled.

"Let's see, other than the usual, 'Where are you from? What do you do?' we talked about entertainment stuff, what kind of music we like, what movies we want to see, things like that."

"That sounds nice. So what's the verdict on him? You seem happy but not smitten."

Together, Jen and Claire filled a pastry bag with their finished frosting, then squeezed a swirl of the sweet cream cheese mixture onto each golden cupcake.

"I guess I'd have to say, over all it was a fun night out. He was cute and laid-back, but there was no real spark. I liked him, but I didn't find myself wondering if he would kiss me at the end of the date. I'd definitely go out with him again, but in the end, I think I see it taking more of a friendship route."

"Too bad."

"The way I see it, it just gives me more dating experience. Plus, it was still a nice evening out," Claire replied.

"That's true. So did he kiss you at the end of the night?"

"Just on the cheek. Sort of how you'd kiss a

relative. Another reason I'm feeling just a friendship." Claire looked down at their nearly completed desserts. "Well, should we get our area cleaned up?"

"Yeah, just let me finish putting the honey drizzle on this last cupcake. These are going to be delish."

Together the pair packed their treats into two to-go containers, as they waited for their sink to fill with hot soapy water. One by one, Claire dropped the load of dirty dishes into the suds for Jen to scrub clean.

"Oh, I meant to ask you," Jen remembered, "I was talking to my Mom today, and she wants to know if you'd like to have brunch on Sunday."

"For sure," Claire agreed with enthusiasm, taking a rinsed mixing bowl from Jen and drying it. "I know it's only been a month or so, but it seems like ages since I had Sunday brunch with your family. What are your parents up to?"

"Actually, my Mom told me today that they are planning another long camping trip." Jen passed a cleaned whisk and spatula to her friend.

"Cool. Where are they going?"

"Out west. They don't have any specific destinations yet. She just told me they felt it had been too long since they threw the tent in the truck and went out on an adventure."

"Your parents are so cool. How long are they going to be gone?"

"She figures about a month, but you know them,

with no real plan it could be more, could be less."

Claire stopped the drying of her utensils, and looked at her.

"What?" Jen giggled self-consciously.

"I just forget sometimes." Claire looked warmly at her friend before resuming her drying.

"Forget what?"

"The kind of family you come from." She shrugged. "It's just so different from most people. Your parents are so happy, and totally in love. It's no wonder you're looking for that, too."

Jen's phone vibrated in her jeans pocket, interrupting their conversation and startling her. Wiping her hands on a dish towel, she then pulled it from her pocket and checked the number.

"Who is it?

Jen frowned. "Not sure."

"Oh. Maybe it's a guy!" Claire leaned in excitedly.

"Let's see." Jen lifted her shoulders and bit her lower lip with anticipation.

"Hello?"

"Hi, Jen. This is Steve."

"Oh, umm, hi," was all Jen could muster. Shocked he was giving her a second call, she put her hand over the phone and whispered to Claire. "Steve."

Claire crossed her arms and forced out an exasperated sigh then added an eye roll to make sure her feelings were getting across.

Jen turned away, stifling a laugh.

"Listen, I know we just went out yesterday, but I was wondering if you are free Tuesday evening for dinner."

"Well, yes. Yes I am." Jen toyed with a sponge on the counter.

"That's great. Would six o'clock work for you?"

"Yes, six is fine. Where will we be going?"

"I'm not sure yet. Somewhere casual, I guess."

"Okay, thanks. I guess I'll see you at six on Tuesday then."

"Yeah, see ya then. Bye."

"Bye."

Jen pressed the off button on the phone, and slid it into her pocket before turning back around.

"Ugh. If I'd known that was Steve, I wouldn't have let you answer it. Sorry."

"Don't be. We're going out to dinner again next week."

"I was afraid of that."

"He's not that bad. I said I'd give him a second chance, remember."

"I know, but if I knew he was going to be such a bum, I would have found someone else. You're way too good for him."

"Well, thanks, but I figure one more date couldn't hurt. Who knows, maybe he was just nervous and it will end up being great. If not, then like you say, at least it's dating practice."

"That's true." She shrugged. "Well, we better finish getting our station cleaned up." Claire stacked the dried mixing bowls in the cupboard below their counter.

"Hey, if you didn't suspect it was Steve, who were you hoping was calling?"

"I thought it might be that guy you work with," Claire answered, as she pulled on her coat.

"Nate?"

"What? No. Who's Nate?"

"The DJ."

"Oh, yeah, nice teeth, average guy. No, I was hoping it was Matty."

"I should've known." Jen shook her head, smiling at her friend's predictability.

CHAPTER SEVEN

*W*ow, *five thirty already.* Jen reached over to shut off her alarm clock.

Saturday had come again, and it was time to shoot another wedding.

If today goes anything like my earlier meetings with the couple, or the rehearsal last night, I am in for an interesting day. She rubbed her eyes sleepily and tried to get herself motivated for the day ahead.

Throughout her meetings with Lisa and Derek, the bride and groom, Jen found herself dealing, not with them, but rather, with Lisa's mother. It wasn't because Lisa and Derek didn't have opinions or ideas, but because her mother made it clear that her own opinions were the right ones, and, in turn, the only ones to be considered. During all the planning, the couple allowed her to completely disregard their wishes, and also insult the things that they had come up with. It was beyond Jen's comprehension why two people would be so willing to let someone step all over what would normally be "their day". As always, she tried to keep the same mindset of "to each his own," and, in the process, seek the desires of the bride and groom while, as respectfully as possible, hush the bride's mother.

Jen made her way into the living room to turn on the TV and check the weather for the day. The sky outside the large window was dark. Regardless of the fact that the month of April had arrived, a winter wind was blowing outdoors and beating against the glass. Quickly she pressed mute on the remote to avoid waking her roommate with the sound. After flipping up a few channels, she landed on one with the day's weather running along the bottom.

31 degrees! Guess I'm dressing warm today.

By six-thirty Jen was showered, dressed, and ready to begin loading up her car. As winter still appeared to be in full swing, she opted to leave her hair down and wavy around her face, a style that always made her feel warm and cozy. She slipped her long coat on over her gray trousers and black V-neck sweater that cinched nicely at her waist.

Knowing her equipment couldn't all be carried at once, and wanting to make as little noise as possible, Jen took all of the necessary things, set them in the hall, and closed the door behind her. After two trips up and down the stairs, she was ready to leave for the salon, where she planned to meet Lisa and her bridesmaids.

The wind was bitterly cold against her bare face

as she removed the needed items from her trunk, prior to entering the building. Shivering, she pushed open the door to the serene spa. Breathing in and out, she began to relax as she allowed the sound of trickling fountains and new age music warm her from the inside out.

"Finally!" Jen heard a sharp and annoyed voice. An overly tanned woman with curly and poorly highlighted hair approached her.

Mother of the bride. Jen bristled at the sound of her voice. She checked her watch to ensure she was in fact as early as she had planned to be before she turned around to face her accuser.

"Good morning, Mrs. Mills." She tried her best to respond in a tone more pleasant than what she was feeling. "Is there a problem? According to my schedule, the girls aren't set to arrive here for another ten minutes."

"Yes, but if I'm not on top of people, they're always late."

"Well, it's an important day. I'm sure they'll all be here shortly. In the meantime, I'll be setting up my things and taking some miscellaneous photos while we wait."

Jen escaped Mrs. Mills as fast as she could and occupied herself by taking pictures of the various colors of nail polish, hair care displays, and anything a fair distance from the woman who was already trying her patience.

"We're here," Lisa called when she and her three bridesmaids entered the salon and spa.

Mrs. Mills rounded the corner towards her daughter. "Oh, Lisa, I can't believe you came here looking like that."

"Mom, what's wrong with this?" She looked her outfit over for blemishes.

"You look like a slob. You know you're getting pictures taken here, right? Is this how you want to be remembered? In sweats?"

Lisa, who was wearing a dark blue pair of high-end yoga pants and a light blue zipper hoodie, looked, at least in Jen's mind, more than presentable for a 7:00 a.m. hair appointment.

"The hairdresser told me I needed to wear something I didn't have to pull over my head, Otherwise my hair might get messed up...Sorry." Her head dropped, defeated.

"Ugh." Her mother grunted, and walked away.

Lisa's face brightened and relaxed as she turned back to her friends and continued their conversation. Jen snapped a few candid pictures of the girls in their excitement before five stylists, one each for the bride, her bridesmaids, and her mother, called them over to begin doing their hair.

Lisa's stylist showed her to a chair. "All right, are you all ready for your big day?"

"Sure am." She looked back at her in the mirror.

"So, we're going with what we practiced last week, right? Except, have you decided which accents you want put into your hair?" The woman fluffed Lisa's freshly washed tresses as she spoke.

"Yeah, I like these pins with the rhinestones on them."

"Those are cute," Jen chimed in. "Mind if I get a picture of them?"

"No, please do." She laid the set of pins down on the hand-held mirror on the counter in front of her.

With the exception of a few comments and shouts from Mrs. Mills, claiming she'd "be bald by the end of the day, should the hairdresser keep combing like that" or complaining of "plastic hair" due to the use of too many products, the first hour passed uneventfully. Jen took photos of each of the ladies, making sure to capture the whole process, from loose down locks to perfectly polished up-dos.

"What are you putting in her hair?" Mrs. Mills demanded of the woman working on Lisa, when her own stylist had finished.

"Mom, those are the pins I want to wear."

"You're going to have a veil on. You won't even see them."

"All right," Lisa conceded. "I guess let's just put on the veil." She cast a disappointed glance back at the woman styling her hair.

"She's putting on her veil," one of the bridesmaids cried out when the hairdresser reached for it.

The three girls surrounded their friend and watched as the stylist slyly slipped one of the rhinestone-covered pins into her hand and used it to pin her veil in place.

"Lisa, you look so beautiful." The maid of honor sighed.

"Just amazing."

"Totally gorgeous," the other two acceded.

The three girls pulled their soon-to-be married friend into a group hug, just as Jen pressed the shutter button on her camera to capture the moment.

"Oh, my daughter," Mrs. Mills called out with false sincerity, as she came toward her. "Watch it. You'll mess up her hair." Her harsh voice returned as she snapped at the bridesmaids and slapped away their arms as she moved in to hug her daughter.

* * * * *

"All right, you're all set." The receptionist told Lisa, handing her the receipt for the services she and her friends had paid for. "Thank you for coming in. I hope your wedding is wonderful."

"Thanks so much," Lisa and all her friends chimed in together.

Before leaving, Jen took one last shot of the four young ladies together, with their hair, nails, and makeup all completed.

"I'll see you at the church," Jen told Lisa.

"Great. See you there." She waved before stepping out into the wind, doing her best to protect her hair, and climbed quickly into their waiting limo.

"Here, you could probably use something to help you get through the day," Jen heard a kind voice say.

She turned around and saw Lisa's stylist holding a large cup of coffee and a handful of creamers and sugar.

"Sorry I don't have something a little stronger to put in it," she joked. "You'll need it dealing with that poor girl's mother."

"Thanks so much." Jen chuckled, gratefully, as she took the warm cup from her hand.

"Good luck," the girl called to her, as Jen headed toward the door.

"Thanks. I'll need it." She lifted her cup in appreciation. "Have a good day."

* * * * *

The following few hours at the church were, for the bride, much quieter and more laid-back than the previous ones had been. Mrs. Mills had taken it upon herself to analyze and then complain about every detail of the wedding as it arrived. First, she yelled at the florist, claiming the roses were not the exact shade of peach that they had discussed, and that arriving five minutes early, as they had done, would certainly cause the blooms to wilt before her only daughter walked down the aisle. Next, she told the pianist that regardless of the fact that he was off to the side of the sanctuary, and could barely be seen, he should have opted for a tuxedo rather than the black suit that he had chosen to wear. Lastly, while walking past the church offices on the way to take pictures of the groom Jen swore she overheard Mrs. Mills lecturing the pastor on the length of his sermon.

Jen knocked on the door of the room where the groom and his friends were waiting.

"It's Jen, the photographer, is everybody decent?"

"Yep, come on in." Derek opened the door for her.

"Hey, there. Are you ready to take some pictures?"

"Sure."

The usual introductions were given, and Jen arranged Derek and his groomsmen up for the photos. After taking a few pictures of them standing side by side, sitting on a bench, or shaking hands, Derek's mother entered with the boutonnieres.

"Hi, Mom."

"Oh, look at my boy, all grown up." She had genuine tears of joy in her eyes as she hugged her son.

"Excuse me." Jen stepped in when the hug was finished. "Could I get a picture of you putting the boutonniere on your son?"

"Absolutely. Do I look all right?" She smoothed her dress nervously.

"Just lovely," Jen assured her.

After finishing a few more photos with the men, Jen excused herself and headed back to the room where Lisa and her friends were. Inside, they were lounging, still in their sweats, sitting on the floor in a circle while they munched on a torn up loaf of French bread and two opened bags of cheese cubes.

"Do you mind if I take some shots of your gown before you put it on?" Jen held up her camera.

"No, not at all," Lisa replied, and continued chatting with her friends. "You have no idea how glad I am going to be to get out of my mother's control. I keep telling myself, just one more day. She has been driving me crazy my entire life, but this wedding has made her worse than ever. She can't let me do anything without trying to make it her way."

Jen listened as she hung the dress on a wall hook, and captured some images of the intricate beading.

"What's your mother-in-law like?" one bridesmaid asked.

"She's so great. Totally supportive of me and Derek, and best of all, she minds her own business."

Jen changed the angle at which she was taking the dress photos and adjusted to take in the entire gown, thinking all the while of how glad she was for Lisa, who was about to enter into what seemed to be a much more pleasant family.

"Looks like it's time for you to get dressed." The

maid of honor suggested to Lisa after checking the time on her phone.

The three bridesmaids changed into their floor length strapless dresses and were ready to help the bride. Carefully, they rested the skirt of her gown on the floor, creating a hole for her to step into. Once Lisa changed into her corset, she stood in the center of her dress and let her friends pull it up and zip it around her. The full tulle skirt, which hit exactly at her hip, paired with the complex details of the bodice, created the perfect princess look. All the while, Jen captured moments of the ladies enjoying the day as they got Lisa ready to meet her groom.

* * * * *

The sky still showed signs of a winter storm when Jen left the church for the Ivy Manor. Afternoon neared its end, and evening approached, though since it had been so overcast all day, each hour seemed like all the ones before.

Bundling herself up as best she could, she gathered her things and ran toward the immense doors, squinting her eyes against the cutting wind. The evening wedding would be downstairs in the smaller reception hall. *That will be perfect for a day like today.* Jen made her way down the steps.

While certainly not as large as the grand ballroom, the smaller hall comfortably allowed for one hundred fifty people, and made every affair feel more intimate with its cozy ski lodge-like charm. The tables of eight were each covered with white linens, a centerpiece of peach roses, and a number of tea light candles. Every white chair cover held in place by a matching peach bow.

Jen wove her way between the tables and chairs, as she carried her equipment towards the back of the room to the staff table.

Oh good, the fire's already lit.

After putting her things down, Jen sat on the large stone hearth. She closed her eyes and listened to the crackling logs, as the flames warmed her up.

Thump.

Jen gasped, jolted out of her relaxed state, and turned her head toward the other side of the room, where the noise had come from.

"Hey. It's just me," Nate reassured her when he saw Jen.

"Oh, hi." Though she didn't know who she had been expecting to see, she felt suddenly glad it was him.

"It's crazy cold out there, isn't it?" Nate came nearer to the fire and warmed his hands.

"I know. It's completely ridiculous for April."

"My thoughts exactly," Nate agreed.

He took off his coat and hung it, along with a garment bag, on the back of a chair at the staff table. Jen moved down the hearth, making room for him.

"Thanks." He sat down on the other end of the stone. "You're here early." He checked his watch.

"Yeah, the weather made for a change of plans. Seeing as how the bride and groom didn't want to be blue in their wedding pictures, they decided to skip the outside stuff."

"Haha. That's probably for the best. So did everything go all right for you the first half of the day?" Nate blew warm air into his hands.

"It was okay." Jen glanced around the room, being sure they were alone. "The mother of the bride is, how should I say this..."

"A beast," he finished for her.

"Yes." Jen laughed. "I was trying to be a bit more tactful, but now that you've said it, yes, a beast. She's awful. I'm assuming you've met her."

"Mmm hmm." Nate nodded. "In case I wasn't already on edge, running stuff on my own for the first time, she really puts the pressure on."

"Are you nervous about DJing?" Jen was surprised

"Definitely."

"But you're so good. You always seem so calm."

"Well, thanks, but the last couple of times I wasn't alone. Uncle Al was always the one in charge. I was just helping. It's a different mindset." He shrugged a shoulder.

"Didn't he say you'd done this before?"

"Yeah, I did, but it was quite a while ago, and, I don't know... Don't you ever get worried before a wedding?"

"I guess I do. Sometimes, I'll have nightmares that I miss an important moment of a ceremony. Or occasionally, when people come to pick up their pictures, I'll have this moment of panic, and worry that they'll open the box of proofs and hate every single one."

"Does that happen a lot?" Nate teased, as he scrunched up his nose and nodded his head in pretend pity.

"No." Jen dropped her jaw in mock offense, and playfully hit his arm with the back of her hand. "I was going to offer to help you get set up, but after that comment, maybe I'll just relax here by the fire for the next couple of hours."

"Well, if that's the case, then I sincerely apologize." Nate laughed, and, getting up from the hearth, offered Jen his hand to help her.

"Apology accepted." She took his hand and stood up. "So, now what can I do?"

"Well, you could start by picking up that speaker and bringing it over here."

Jen looked in the direction Nate had pointed, and upon seeing the four-foot tall electronic, immediately began to sit back down.

"I'm just kidding." Nate looked amused as he

caught her hands and pulled her back up before she could take her seat again. "It's on wheels. We can push it."

* * * * *

The next hour flew by. Jen pulled her hair back in a loose ponytail to keep it out of her eyes as they worked together, moving equipment. Once everything was where it needed to be, they plugged in the laptop, sub-woofer, and each speaker, to the appropriate outlet or place on the mixer.

"Looks like we're all set. Now we just need to test it out and make sure we've got everything right. What song should I play?" Nate scrolled through an endless playlist of mp3s.

Jen moved to look at the list, too.

"Oh. How about one of those great father daughter songs. I love those." She tried to keep a straight face.

"Very funny." Nate chuckled. "Do you have another preference?"

"Wait, stop. How about that one? Twilight Nocturne." She pointed to a big band instrumental.

"An excellent choice." Nate nodded.

"Thank you."

An understated string bass slowly and softly plucked out notes. Soon a brass quartet joined in and the reception hall was filled with sound.

Nate adjusted levels on the mixer, and Jen

stepped to the center of the room to listen.

"Sounds good," she called to him.

"What is this terrible song?"

Immediately, Jen and Nate knew the bride's mother had arrived. Jen swiftly pulled the elastic out of her hair and dusted off her black sweater, trying to make herself look as neat as possible. Nate abruptly stopped the music.

"That was not on the list of songs I gave you. Why would you..." Mrs. Mills trailed off, as her attention suddenly turned to the tables. "What are these roses doing here?" she demanded, looking at Jen.

"I'm not sure. They've been here since I arrived." Jen bit down on her lip, instantly regretting her choice of words.

"They have been here *how* long?"

Nate appeared at Jen's side. "She meant we haven't been here all that long, and the florist had probably just finished setting up before we came. Peach is a very nice color choice. Did you pick that?"

"Of course I did. If it were up to Lisa, who knows what horrendous colors we'd have in here. Where is that girl, anyway?"

This time, before either Jen or Nate could attempt to answer, Mrs. Mills pulled a cell phone from her purse and exited the room, no doubt trying to keep tabs on her daughter.

"Whew. Thanks." Relief washed over Jen.

"No problem. This is going to be quite a night." He sighed. "For the record, I hate peach."

With that, the mood lightened, and the two laughed.

* * * * *

Later that evening, the cocktail hour was in full swing. Guests were mingling with each other, drinks in hand, as they noshed on stuffed mushroom caps, crab cakes, and assorted cheeses.

Jen snapped photos of couples enjoying the evening together and relatives catching up after years apart.

She checked her watch and noticed it was nearly time for Lisa and Derek to arrive and so left the reception hall to wait for them. A few minutes later, and exactly on time, the newly married couple came in.

"Hi, love birds." Jen beamed. "Are you ready for your entrance?"

"Sure are." The pair glowed as they looked at each other.

"Great. I'll go in and let them know you're ready."

Jen did as she said, and a moment later, the entrance music that Mrs. Mills had selected played throughout the hall. Nate faded it down a bit and made the introductions. One by one, the three bridesmaids and groomsmen walked in, the first couple clapping to the music, the next stopping to do a quick twirl on the dance floor, and finally the best man and maid of honor came in, cheering and riling up the guests for when Lisa and Derek would make their grand entrance.

"And now, ladies and gentlemen," Nate began, his smooth voice sounding clearly over the music, "it's my pleasure to introduce to you, for the first time, Mr. and Mrs. Derek Spooner."

The hall erupted with applause and cheers as Derek carried Lisa in piggyback. She shook her bouquet in the air.

"Turn this down, right now," Mrs. Mills yelled. "Put on something slower. I can't have my daughter acting like this. She looks ridiculous."

"Whatever you say."

Jen cast Nate a sympathetic look.

Soon after, Lisa and Derek took their seats at the head table. Guests followed suit and did the same at their own round tables. As always, the bar emptied, and Jen took the opportunity to get her usual beverage, cranberry juice with a slice of lime.

"Hey, I'm gonna get something to drink, do you want anything?" she asked Nate.

"That'd be great. Could you get me a pop?"

"Sure. Be right back."

Matty gave Jen a winning grin as she approached the bar. "I was wondering when you were going to come over here. What can I get to drink for the hottest girl here?"

"Seriously, Matty? Does that work on anybody?" She sat down on a stool, resting her arms on the bar top.

"All the time. You're just playing hard to get."

He reached under the counter and slyly lifted a rather full whiskey glass to his lips.

"So, what would you like?" Matty put his hand on hers and drew little circles on the inside of her wrist with his index finger.

"A pop and my usual." She pulled her arm away. "You're unbelievable."

"That's what they tell me," he joked, as he poured the drinks she requested and put them on the bar.

"Thanks." She got up and turned to go.

"You're just going to take your drinks and run? You don't want to stay a while?"

"Tempting as that offer is, I have work to do, and so do you."

"No fun, as always," Matty called after her.

"Hey. Here ya go." Jen handed Nate his beverage.

"Thanks." He took a quick drink, then set his glass down on the staff table nearby. "And thanks, by the way, for setting everything up with me. That was a huge help."

"Anytime," she replied with sincerity. "Looks like Angie's bringing our food out. Wanna eat?"

"Absolutely." Nate pulled a dining chair out for

Jen. "So are you working the wedding next weekend?"

"Thank you." She sat down. "No, I'm not. Al and Frankie tried to get me the gig, but I guess a relative of the groom is a photographer for one of the papers, so he'll be shooting it."

"Aww. Too bad."

"Not really. It's nice, every once in a while when I have a free Saturday. Plus, it will give me a week without picture editing, and I'll be able to get some paperwork done.

"I meant too bad for me. What am I supposed to do without the free labor to help me set up?" he joked.

"Well, I did do all the work. You'll pretty much be lost without me here," she teased. "Seriously though, without Al being here, do you want my number in case you need help with anything?"

"That'd be great. Thanks."

They both pulled out their cell phones, Nate from his pocket and Jen reaching into her purse.

"What's your last name?" Jen realized she didn't know it.

"Smith. What's yours?"

"Schuman."

"Pleasure to meet you, Miss Schuman." He nodded once, as he put a napkin in his lap.

"You as well, Mr. Smith. You as well."

CHAPTER EIGHT

*T*uesday *night. 6:15 p.m., still no sign of Steve.*
Though she was annoyed with the wait, this time around Jen's nerves were much more under control. Sitting on the couch, flipping back and forth between a cooking show and one on home renovation, she let her mind wander. It surprised her how little she had thought about her date as she edited pictures throughout the day. The few times it did come to her mind, it was more of a thing to do, rather than a thing to daydream about. Maybe it was the fact that the request for a second date was an affirmation that he liked her, or the idea that she was doing this for dating practice, and not because she was all that into him. Whatever it was, though, while it certainly left something to be desired in the excitement and butterflies department, Jen felt that at least it was something to do on an evening otherwise devoid of plans.

Five minutes later, the buzzer rang.

Jen stood up and walked over to it.

"Hello?"

"Hey. It's Steve. Can you come down?"

"Be right there."

A little put off by the fact that he didn't want to bother coming up to get her, Jen reminded herself that she was keeping an open mind and giving him a second chance.

Before leaving the apartment, she gave herself a last once-over in the mirror. Her skinny jeans and colorful, layered long and short sleeved T's were in her usual quirky, casual style, and the front braid she had put in her hair made her feel a little more dressed up. *Perfect,* she thought, and headed down the stairs.

When she reached Steve at the front door Jen put on a cheerful expression.

"Hi. It's good to see you again." She stuck out a hand.

"You, too." He ignored her palm and hugged her instead.

A short, awkward silence filled the foyer as Jen waited, half expecting him to apologize, or at least acknowledge in some way, the fact that he was twenty minutes late.

"Well, let's go," Steve prompted after a moment, never mentioning the time, and opened the door to go outside.

Like their last date, he opened the driver's side door, first ignoring Jen's. Once they were both inside, she commenced their conversation.

"So, have you decided where we're going to eat?"

"Just down the road to Buddie's Diner. Do you know it?"

Remembering Claire's awful date there a few weeks earlier, Jen replied with a chuckle. "Yes. Yes, I do"

"What's so funny?"

"Oh, Claire just had a bad date there recently, that's all."

"Well, let's hope ours is better." Steve put his chubby hand on Jen's.

Normally, handholding was a thing Jen would be all for on a second date, but something about it being Steve's hand made it far less appealing. Thankful that he lifted it to turn on the rear defrost, Jen took the opportunity to intertwine her own fingers and put her hands in her lap.

"Here we are," Steve announced after driving a block down the road.

"Great."

Jen hopped out of the car right away, having learned from experience that Steve was not the door-opening type.

Buddie's was crowded and noisy, but in a pleasant and friendly kind of way. Not being a restaurant for the health conscience, it offered the menu of a typical greasy spoon establishment. The smell of garlic toast and spaghetti were heavy in the air that evening.

"Looks like it's all you can eat Italian night," Jen commented when they entered the door.

Steve had nothing to add to this, so instead stood silently by her and ran his hand through his sandy brown hair.

"Two this evening?" the young hostess asked.

"Yes. Thanks," Jen replied.

"Right this way." She led them to the first booth near the salad bar and dropped their plastic-covered menus on the table.

"Enjoy your meal," she added before walking away.

Jen and Steve looked over their menus in silence for a few moments.

"I'm totally in the mood for a burger today. What about you?" Jen pointed to the list of burgers and sandwiches Buddie's offered.

"Not sure yet."

"Do you want to share an appetizer in the meantime? Maybe a basket of onion rings or something?"

"No, I don't like to share food with people."

"Oh, okay. That's all right."

A waitress in her early twenties, obviously pregnant, came to their table.

"Do you know what you'd like, or do you need a few minutes?"

"You go ahead," Steve said. "I'll figure out what I want while you order."

"I'll have the five alarm burger with seasoned fries, please."

The waitress smiled and tapped her pen on her pad. "That's so good. I never would've guessed that during pregnancy I'd want spicy food, but this baby cannot get enough of that sandwich. I guess it's a good thing I work here, huh?"

Jen laughed. "At least you're craving something delicious. I'm sure it beats wanting weird combos like pickles and peanut butter."

"Yeah. I'm not gonna lie, the baby isn't the only one who wants that burger; I certainly do enjoy them, too."

"I'll have," Steven interrupted their conversation, "the all-you-can-eat fettuccine alfredo."

"All right." The waitress jotted his order down on her note pad, a hint of annoyance in her voice. "I'll put this right in."

"Great. Thanks," Jen said to the server, and then turned to Steve. "So how was the rest of your week?" She attempted to initiate conversation a second time when the waitress took her leave.

"It was good."

When Steve said nothing else, Jen spoke again.

"I had a wedding this weekend." After no response she continued. "It was a pretty interesting experience." She forced a chuckle.

Jen watched Steve look down at his watch and then proceed to look around the room.

"Mmm hmmm," he mumbled, obviously not listening.

"The bride's mother..." Jen trailed off when she saw Steve's wandering eyes stop and begin to stare at something or someone across the restaurant. Curious as to what he was looking at, she followed his line of sight straight to the chest of a young waitress in a low cut t-shirt, who happened to be leaning forward as she wrote down an order.

Wow. This guy is unbelievable. I'm sitting right here. Wanting to put an end to the uncomfortable stare, she readjusted her position in the booth, and, while uncrossing her legs, intentionally bumped him under the table.

Steve's neck snapped back towards her.

"Yeah, so you must make pretty good money being a photographer, huh?" Steve's eyes wandered back to where the waitress had stood. When it was clear she'd moved into the kitchen, he turned back to Jen, disappointment written all over his face.

Jen never liked the fact that people always assumed she made a lot of money as a photographer, and certainly didn't appreciate being asked about it outright on a second date. She gave her usual response.

"It pays the bills."

It was Jen's turn to look around the restaurant. Between Steve's complete lack of social skills, dry conversation, and eyes for other women, she was certain that he was not someone she wanted to be with in any capacity. Only one thought filled her mind, ending the date as soon as possible. They sat in silence as she watched the customers enjoying their meals. At the salad bar, a man who looked to be a grandfather was helping his granddaughter pick out what toppings she wanted for her greens. A nearby table held a middle-aged man who was offering his wife crushed red pepper and parmesan cheese before sprinkling his own meal with them.

After what seemed like hours to Jen, but in actuality was only minutes, their food arrived.

"Here you go, and here are some extra napkins. Do you need anything else?"

"No," Steve managed to get out before stuffing his mouth with the first bite of the long flat noodles.

"Thank you though," Jen added, trying to counteract some of the rudeness of her dining partner.

Unlike their last shared meal, this time Jen felt no need to make idle chitchat with her date. Instead, she inhaled her burger as fast as she could and tried not to judge as she watched Steve's chubby hands move rapidly from bowl to face, jamming larger and larger forkfuls of pasta into his mouth.

"You ready to go?" Steve looked to Jen.

She had just finished off the last of her fries, and their waitress had, only minutes before, dropped off the check on their table.

"Definitely," Jen responded, aware that her answer may have come a bit too eagerly.

After paying, they got into his black sports car and began the short drive back to Jen's apartment. This time she didn't bother trying to make conversation. To her great surprise, when they arrived at her building, Steve turned off the car and got out.

"I'll walk you to your door," he explained.

Once in the building, Steve went directly to the elevator and pressed the up button.

"What floor is it?"

"Six, but why don't we just take the stairs?"

"Why would I want to walk six flights if I don't have to?" He looked shocked.

"Because it's nice to walk. Because we've got legs, and we might as well use them. Because, I just like to."

"Well, you're welcome to walk all the steps you want, but I'm riding up."

Jen ascended the stairs, taking two steps at a time once she was out of Steve's line of vision. With anyone else, she would have taken the elevator, but after Steve's behavior that evening, Jen's stubbornness got the best of her. When she reached the top, he was leaning against the wall at the entrance to the elevator, arms crossed over his chest.

"See, my way was faster." He wore a smug expression on his face.

"I didn't say my way was faster, I just said I liked taking the stairs." Jen tensed up, trying her best not to pick a fight. "Well, this is me." She jerked her head towards the apartment door. "Thanks for dinner." She put her key into the door.

"Yeah, we should do this again." Steve's tone had changed and he was moving towards her.

Jen backed away, bumping her head on the door. *He has got to be kidding.* Either not noticing that she wasn't interested, or not caring, Steve put one of his hands on the door, and the other on Jen's hip. The smell of his garlic breath wafted toward her nose. As he moved in to kiss her, she was, at the last moment, able to turn her cheek to him, causing his protuberant nose to poke her in the face.

Steve forced a chuckle. "Let's try that again."

"Let's not," Jen said, surprised by her own straightforwardness. She tried her best to maintain a facial expression that matched the confidence in her voice.

Steve pulled back. "Excuse me?" His tone was snarky.

"Listen, I appreciate dinner, but I'm not interested in continuing this. Thanks, though," she added after a pause, not wanting to be rude.

"Well, you could have told me you felt like this before I paid for dinner," Steve retorted.

"If the $6.95 means that much to you, I'll be happy to pay you back right now." With each passing second Jen found herself more and more angry. She dug in her purse for her wallet.

"No. No. I'll be the bigger person here." He put both palms up in defeat. "See ya 'round," Steve grunted, as he returned to the elevator and pressed the down button.

Not waiting to see him get in, Jen opened the door to her apartment, hurried inside, and slammed it behind her. Leaning against the wooden frame, she couldn't help but laugh in disbelief at what just happened.

Sharing a plate of onion rings with a person he likes, he won't do, but kissing someone who clearly isn't interested, that he will.

CHAPTER NINE

*A*ll right, it was 8.2 miles from my house to the *salon, 4.7 from there to the church, 4.1 from the church to the Ivy Manor, and then 6.3 from the Manor back to my house.* Jen typed each number into her mileage log.

It was Wednesday, and considering how well her picture editing for the week had been going, Jen decided to spend the morning at her office in the Manor, sorting through the paperwork that had been piling up. Surrounded by documents splayed all over her meeting table, she searched the internet for the addresses of each of the locations she had traveled to, then entered the last of the digits into her log, before saving her work.

Good to have that done.

Looking around her at the contracts and questionnaires strewn about, Jen began the process of organizing them all, first by date, then each wedding into its own folder, with all the couple's paperwork in a specific order so that she could retrieve the information quickly if ever needed.

Through her opened door, she heard several sets of footsteps coming up the staircase and then step into the office next to hers. The door closed behind them. Jen tapped a stack of papers on the table to straighten them out, listening to the sound of three muffled voices coming through the wall. Though she couldn't hear what any of them were saying, she could make out the sound of one voice she knew to be Nate's.

Must be meeting with a bride and groom.

The couple's voices suddenly rose as a spat broke out between them.

Yes, definitely a bride and groom. She chuckled to herself.

She heard Nate's voice, his tone calm and kind, and the arguing subsided.

Jen continued organizing her documents, all the while thinking about her earlier conversation with Nate, and the difficulties of working in the wedding industry.

Poor guy. His least favorite part. This meeting seems particularly arduous. I wonder who'll win out, the groom or the bride.

After several more minutes of working, Jen finally put the last of her papers away and closed the cabinet drawer. Nate's voice interrupted her thoughts, this time clear.

"It was a pleasure meeting you both. I look

forward to the big day. If you have any questions between now and then, my contact information is in the folder I gave you. Feel free to call with anything you need."

"Thank you," a woman's voice said.

"Have a good one," followed the man's.

A short silence followed that Jen imagined was filled with the usual, deal closing handshakes. She heard the guests exiting the building, and then quick footsteps made their way back up the spiraling staircase.

"Hey, you." Nate grinned as he leaned against the doorframe of Jen's office. "I thought I heard you working up here. Hope we didn't disturb you."

"No. Not at all. That sounded like quite a meeting, though."

"Nah, they weren't too bad." He gave casual a wave of his hand. "I was just about to get some lunch, between my meetings. Wanna come?"

"Sure, I'm just about done here. Give me a minute to finish up."

"Cool. I'll go get my jacket."

Jen shut down her laptop, put her fitted jacket on over her t-shirt, and shut off the lights. When she met Nate back in the hall he was pulling his sports jacket on over his striped dress shirt.

"You all set?" He closed the office door behind him.

"Yep."

The two made their way down the staircase together.

"Where do you want to go?" he inquired.

"Hmm. Well, this place, near where I live, Java Jane's, has started serving paninis, and I've been dying to try them. How does that sound?"

"Sounds great. Just tell me how to get there."

They reached the bottom of the stairs. Nate opened the door and ushered Jen out before him.

Retrieving his keys from his jacket pocket, he tossed them into his opposite hand and clicked the unlock button before opening the passenger side door for her.

"Thanks," Jen said.

They both hopped in the SUV and Nate started it up, heading towards the exit of the parking lot as he clicked his seat belt into place.

"Which way?"

"Left up here."

Once a car or two had passed, Nate pulled out into the road.

Jen watched him as he drove. "So who's your next meeting with?"

"Emma and Aaron, I think," he replied.

"Oh, they are so great. Have you met them yet?"

"Yeah. Just briefly. They seem good together. I'm thinking it should be a breeze today when we go over details of what they want to have played and when."

"I'm sure it will be. They were an absolute dream for me to work with."

Their conversation about various couples and the people who worked at the Ivy Manor, sprinkled with driving directions from Jen, continued as they traveled.

"It's right in this plaza here." Jen pointed as they approached their lunch destination.

The aroma of coffee and fresh bread wafted towards their noses as they entered the doors of the establishment.

"Mmm. Smells good." He took an appreciative deep breath.

"Sure does."

Java Jane's was small and cozy. Pale wooden tables, some with chessboards inlaid in their tops, and matching pale wooden chairs filled the tiny space, the largest of which held only four people. Along the walls, hung by wires, were drawings, paintings, and photographs created by local artists.

Together Jen and Nate approached the counter and gazed up at the chalk-written menu that hung on the brick behind it.

"Wow, a lot of these sound good," Nate commented.

"Yeah, I don't know if I want the avocado turkey or the French dip."

"Want to get both and split 'em? That way we can taste more than one," Nate suggested.

"Sounds good to me."

"You ready to order?" the green apron clad girl at the counter asked Nate and Jen.

"I think so," Nate began. "Can we please have the avocado turkey panini, a French dip panini, and..." He looked to Jen. "What would you like to drink?"

"Umm, I'll have a tall toffee frappe," she answered.

"Yeah, one of those," Nate confirmed to the cashier. "And a grande coffee with cream, the house blend."

"All right. Would you like homemade chips or salads with your sandwiches?"

"Chips," Nate and Jen answered in unison, laughing after doing so.

"That will be $18.96."

Nate pulled out his wallet and handed her a $20.

"Thanks, but you don't have to do that. I can at least pay for my part," Jen offered.

"Nah, don't worry about it. This way when I eat all my food, and then half of yours, I won't have to feel bad about it," he joked.

"Well, you're gonna have to fight me for it."

Nate dropped a few singles into the coffee cup marked "tips," and the two moved down the counter to where their finished food would be set out.

"So, you mentioned you live around here; do you come here often?"

"Quite a bit. I live in the apartments across that side street." Jen gestured through a set of windows.

"Order's up." A man, also sheathed in a green apron, bellowed from behind the counter as he put their lunch on top of it.

"Thanks." Nate reached for the tray. "Where do you want to sit?"

"How about over there." Jen pointed, and walked toward a two top under a water color painting.

Nate set the tray down on the table as Jen took a seat.

"Should we divvy them up now?" Nate suggested.

"Sure."

He took the basket nearest to him containing the French dip sandwich, put one of the gooey cheesy halves into Jen's basket, and placed the dish of au jus in the center of the table. Jen then took a half of the turkey avocado and handed it to Nate.

"Oh, wow," Nate exclaimed after dunking and chewing his first bite of the beefy panini. "This is a good sandwich."

"So is this." Jen munched the juicy turkey and creamy avocado combination appreciatively. "Great idea splitting them."

"So, do you live by yourself?" Nate picked up a

chip.

"No. I have a roommate. Her name's Claire. She's the best. Like the sister I never had."

"Yeah? How so?" Nate looked at her, showing interest.

"We're just close and we get along great. She's super thoughtful, and kind, and *really* funny, so that makes it easy to be around her."

"She sounds great. So then, do you have any brothers, or are you an only child?"

Jen swallowed a bite of the French dip. "Only child. What about you? Do you have any siblings? Are you as close with the rest of your family as you are with Al?"

"Yep. I'm close with my whole family. I have an older sister named Susan. She's married. My brother-in-law, John, is a great guy. Such a good match for Suz. They have a daughter named Ruby. Wanna see her?" Nate took his wallet out of his pocket and produced a small photo.

He handed Jen the picture of his niece. "She's four."

"Oh my goodness, she's adorable," Jen cooed.

"Yeah, we all think so. And she's so fun." He took back the picture, and, after looking at it again, placed it carefully in its spot in his wallet.

"So what about your parents? Since it's just you and them, do you guys have a good relationship?"

"Mmm hmm." Jen nodded, as she took a sip of her frappe. "They're amazing people, both as individuals and as a couple."

"In what ways?" Nate looked intently across the table at her.

"Well, for one, they're both artistic."

"So that's where you get it from."

"Yep. We're a lot alike in that sense, but they're way more adventurous. They have this undying desire to experience and learn all kinds of different things. Like, this weekend, they'll be packing up the truck and traveling around the country for a month, maybe more, just sleeping wherever they see fit and going wherever the road takes them."

"They sound fun."

"They are." Jen dunked her French dip.

"How long have they been married?"

"Almost thirty-five years. Which I think is pretty amazing for anybody, but especially people who are as free-spirited as them." She paused, thinking for a moment. "I think when two people want to live life to the fullest like that, even though it might be satisfying, the temptation is there to just do what *you* want and kind of forget about the other person, you know?"

"I can see that. So was that a problem in your family?"

"No. That's why I think my parents are such a

good match. They put the other person first all the time."

"That's important."

"I agree," Jen concurred with enthusiasm. "If a person wants to do their own thing, that is totally fine, but I don't see the need to be in a relationship then."

"Absolutely. So what about you?"

"What *about* me?"

"Are you in a relationship, or are you happy doing your own thing?"

"Well, neither." Jen shrugged. "I mean, I'm not in a relationship, but not because I want to do my own thing."

Nate took a sip of his coffee as he listened.

"Claire thinks it's good to date for fun, and for dating practice, which for some people it is, but I don't think it's for me."

"You're more of the relationship type?" He put down his cup.

"Yeah. What about you?"

"I like being in a relationship, too, when it's the right person."

"So do you have a girlfriend now?"

"Nope. I think it's hard to carry on a relationship when you're gone every weekend. Most girls expect that to be couple time, and rightfully so. That's how most people date."

Jen couldn't believe her ears.

"Exactly. Most people don't get that. Working those days can be tough." She waited a beat before continuing. "So, if you don't mind me asking, what about before life at the Ivy Manor, any significant ladies from that time in your life?" Jen teased.

"Nah." He waved a chip in his hand. "Nothing serious, at least. I never had much of a chance."

"What do ya mean?" Jen stopped eating to listen more intently.

Nate gave a sheepish chuckle when he saw her waiting with rapt attention.

"You really want to hear this?" He looked uncertain.

"Yeah!" Jen leaned forward to urge him on.

He raised his shoulders bashfully. "Well, after college, I helped Al with the DJ thing. He was preparing to make me part of the business, which, don't get me wrong, I appreciated, and still do." He gestured with his hands as if to hold back any of her doubts. "At that time I felt like spending my days sleeping in, and spending my weekends playing music wasn't the best use of, well, me. I felt bad."

"So, what *was* the best use of you?"

"Well, I figured I was young, and able to work, and there are so many people out there who aren't able to even do the work around their own homes, so I joined a volunteer labor force. I traveled with them around the country for a few years."

"Really? That's amazing. What kind of work did you do?"

"All kinds of things. We repaired houses that were damaged in storms, or were just getting old and couldn't be kept up by the owner. We planted gardens, helped on farms. Stuff like that."

Jen found herself staring at Nate, in awe of what she just learned about him, and the fact that he talked about it so nonchalantly, as if everyone spent years thinking of others rather than themselves.

"Were you happy?"

"Absolutely."

"What made you come back, then?"

"It was always the plan for me to come back at some point. I knew Uncle Al, not having his own kids, was going to need help with at least a portion of the business. Plus, my family is here. I always stayed in close contact with them, but I missed being around them. That was the hardest part about being away for that long."

"I can't even imagine that. You are so selfless."

"Nah." He gave a humble wave. "I was doing what I wanted to do. And I enjoyed it."

"Do you enjoy your life now, too?"

"For sure. More than ever, in fact. That was a great time, and I'm so glad I did it, but setting up a life here is what I want to do now. Being away made me appreciate that even more."

"I'm glad for you," she said. "So, now that you're here, and since Al will be back from his trip next week, what does that mean for you and the Manor?"

"Actually, I'm going to be staying on with the Ivy Manor for a while."

Jen didn't know why, but a rush of relief ran through her at the sound of his words.

"Excellent."

"Thanks. I'm happy about it, too."

A comfortable lull in the conversation allowed them to finish their meal.

"This was great," he commenced when their plates were empty. "The food and the company, I mean."

"Thanks. I think so, too. Thanks again for lunch. It was delish."

"Well, shall we?" Nate motioned towards their table, now void of food.

Together they cleaned up, tossing out their napkins and leaving their plates on the counter before heading out the door with the remainder of their drinks in hand.

* * * * *

The ride back to the Manor went quickly, as all the lunch hour traffic had already passed through town. Getting out of Nate's SUV, the pair strolled through the parking lot.

"I should probably go get ready for my next meeting." Nate stopped when they reached the entrance to the Manor.

"Yeah, I've got plenty of unedited pictures awaiting me at home."

"Thanks for coming out. It sure beat eating alone."

"Thanks for taking me. I had so much fun."

"Me, too." Nate beamed. "Well, I'll see you on Saturday."

"See ya then." Jen waved, as they went their separate ways.

* * * * *

Jen was at the stove stirring a pan of fried rice when Claire came home that evening.

"I'm home." Claire dropped her purse on the floor and kicked off her heels.

"How was your day?"

"Busy, but boring. How about yours?"

"It was good. I had lunch with Nate today."

"You had a date? With who?" Claire dashed over to her friend.

"I didn't say date. I said lunch with Nate. It wasn't a date," she repeated.

"Okay." Claire looked skeptically at Jen. "How did that come about?"

"We were both at the Manor. I was just finishing up my work, and he had some time between meetings, so he asked if I wanted to get lunch."

"Where did you go?"

"Java Jane's."

"Did you pick it or did he?"

"I did." Jen retrieved two plates from the cupboard and dished out the fried rice.

"Did you each pay for yourselves?"

"Well, no. He paid."

"So let me get this straight." Claire opened the fridge and removed an iced tea. "He invited you to lunch, he let you pick, and he paid for it, but this wasn't a date?" Claire's tone made it clear she certainly believed it to be one.

"No. We're just friends."

"So you don't like him at all?"

"No, I like him a lot. He's a great guy. It's just, he's more of the friend type. In fact, we were talking about relationships, and he said the same thing I did about dating being so hard when you're…"

Claire bit down on her lip in an attempt to keep the grin from spreading across her face.

"What?"

"Nothing." Claire shook her head and laughed. "Nothing at all."

CHAPTER TEN

Right on time. Jen knocked on the door of the house in front of her.

As in most weddings, the bride wanted pictures of her and her friends getting ready. Instead of going to a salon, all the bridesmaids and women of the family were meeting at the home of the bride's parents. The small brick house was located in a charming neighborhood not too far from the Ivy Manor.

After a long pause, the door swung open.

"Hi." A disheveled but jovial-looking woman greeted her.

"Hello. I'm Jen. The photographer."

"Nice to meet you. I'm Elaine, Stephanie's mother." She offered Jen her hand. "Come on in."

"Thank you."

Once inside, Jen understood the wait to answer the door. It was only 8:00 a.m. and the home, which from the outside appeared to be quaint and quiet, was already a mad house inside. From the entrance, two televisions were visible, both on full blast, one that no one seemed to be watching, and the other surrounded by a group of unruly men. A set of middle-aged women sat gabbing around the kitchen table. Two dogs tore through the living room, barking. A small girl, who Jen presumed to be the flower girl, stood in front of the couch screaming as the tangles were combed out of her hair by a woman who appeared to be her mother.

"Stephanie is in the dining room with her friends," Elaine informed over the sound of the chaos.

"Thanks."

Jen's presence in the dining room wasn't noticed until she tapped Stephanie on the shoulder.

The bride jumped up. "Oh, hi."

Stephanie turned to her friends, "Everyone, this is Jen. She'll be doing the pictures today." Glancing at Jen she asked, "So do you need us to do anything right now?"

"Nope, just act natural. Keep getting ready, and I'll take pictures along the way."

"All right. Want a mimosa?"

"Thanks, but I'm good," Jen declined.

The dining room table, surrounded by Stephanie and her bridesmaids, held an array of beauty products. In front of each girl were a mirror, a variety of makeup, and a cocktail. The center of the table held four empty champagne bottles, two full ones, and an empty carton of orange juice.

Jen tried her best to concentrate despite the noise. The girls at the table were practically yelling their requests for this brush or that eyeliner, just to be heard over the sounds from the other rooms. Every few minutes, a cheer or jeer would erupt from the men in the family room.

Two plump women from the kitchen came into the dining room.

"Do you ladies need another drink in here?"

A hearty yes came from all around the table, and so they opened the last two bottles of champagne and poured some into each girl's glass, this time, minus the orange juice.

"Oh honey, that's enough of these pictures for now," a woman who resembled Stephanie's mother addressed Jen as she was about to take a shot of one bridesmaid applying blush to the cheeks of another. "I'm Steffy's aunt, we need a picture of us together."

The aunt bent down next to her niece, putting her hands on her shoulders and their cheeks together. Both women gave cheesy fake grins, and Jen snapped the picture.

"You should come in here, and make sure you get photos of the entire family. We're never all together like this."

Jen looked at the bride.

"Yeah, that's true. Go ahead."

Jen followed the woman into the kitchen where

the lot of them sat. There, they told her the names and relations of each member of the family.

"It's nice to meet you all. I'm not very good with names," she confessed, "but I'll do my best."

After a few photos in the kitchen, Stephanie's mother and all of the aunts took her around to the other rooms of the house where she met every other member of the family. All the while, Jen captured photos of the group, both posed together and candidly.

"Mom!" Stephanie's voice pierced through the din.

"What?" Elaine yelled in Jen's ear.

Jen tried not to flinch.

"We need more drinks," Stephanie shouted.

Elaine and the aunts left the family room and returned with bottles of beer. It was clear to Jen that if Stephanie and her friends weren't buzzed when she arrived at the house, they were now. She took it as a sign that it was necessary to get the pictures moving. In her experience, Jen had found that couples typically want their wedding photographs to portray the day in the most positive light possible. The more people drank, the harder that became. In situations like this, she knew it was best to get as many pictures as she could early in the day.

Jen looked to the bridesmaids. "Now that you're all finishing up your makeup, would you like to take some pictures together?"

"Sure," Stephanie answered for the group. "I'm going to get my dress on."

"Would you like pictures of that?"

"Nah. It will be faster this way." The bride grabbed a beer and carried it down the hallway to the room where her dress hung.

"All right," Jen initiated, after allowing the bride's family to ooh and ah over her completed look. "Why don't we start with just you?" She led the way out the door and into the front yard.

Jen closed her eyes as she let the quiet of the outdoors engulf her, before turning back to face Stephanie.

"Would you like to do a few on your front steps?" she suggested.

Stephanie was handed her bouquet by one of her bridesmaids, who then cascaded the train of the wedding gown down the front stairs.

"Very nice," Jen encouraged. "On three. One. Two. Three."

Jen snapped the picture as the bride put on an awkward toothy expression.

"Could you hand me my beer?" Stephanie called to the girl closest to her, who happily obliged.

"Want to do another one?" Jen let her take a sip.

"Sure." Giggling, she almost dropped the bottle as she handed it back to her friend.

Jen snapped another shot.

"Wait, I wasn't ready." The bride made a serious, almost angry face, then immediately doubled over with the giggles again, this time her friends following suit.

This is beyond buzzed.

Rapidly hitting the shutter button, Jen took the opportunity to capture a few images of the girls with their heads thrown back in laughter, hoping she could later work them to look like an intimate moment of gladness between friends rather than drunken chortles.

"What do you say to some group shots?" Jen advised.

"Sure." With that, all the ladies of the bridal party dropped down onto the pavement together.

Let's see, how should I do this? Jen contemplated the situation, trying to find the best way to organize the raucous bunch.

"All right, could I please have you scoot over to your left, and our maid of honor, if you could please take a seat on the steps by the bride? That's nice."

The girls all leaned their heads in and smiled for Jen as she took the picture.

"We have wine," a boisterous aunt announced, as the screen door swung open, hitting the bride and her best friend.

The girls all got off the cement and the aunts

poured out the front door, carrying glasses and bottles.

As more drinks were distributed, Jen looked around the yard for a new area to set up photos of the bride with each of her friends. Across the lawn was a cute white picket fence that she thought would do nicely.

"Stephanie, when you're ready, I'd like to take a picture of you with each of your bridesmaids beside that fence."

The entire group made their way to it and stood waiting for instruction.

"All right, Stephanie, lean up against the fence and rest your hand on that post. Yes, that looks lovely. Now, if our maid of honor could join you."

As each girl stepped up with the bride, Jen directed the pair to make sure every picture was different and interesting.

"Maybe take one step to your right. Good. Now look a little bit towards each other."

Between each photo, the ladies continued enjoying their refreshments.

Suddenly, a loud slam pierced the air.

"Now, stay out!" a man in jeans and a stained undershirt threatened from the door.

Before they realized what was going on, the two dogs, who had been running through the house, came charging outside, one after the other, toward the women standing on the lawn. Screams of warning exploded from the group, but it was too late. Turning at the very last second and narrowly missing Stephanie, the dogs ran by, startling her enough to loosen her grip on the wineglass.

Everyone watched in horror. It was like seeing it in slow motion. The glass flew up in the air; the deep red liquid splashed out of it and then splattered all over the front of her white gown.

"NO!" The bride shrieked in disbelief and burst into tears. "You stupid..." Her voice trailed off as she ran, screaming a string of choice words towards the man at the door.

The women left outside talked amongst themselves about the great tragedy that they had just witnessed, as they slowly wandered back to the house.

Jen followed the women into the living room where Stephanie laid on the couch sobbing.

"Honey, don't worry. We can try and get it out." Her mother's once jovial tone had vanished.

"You still look good," her maid of honor tried to reassure her.

Jen stayed at the back of the room, not wanting to be in the way as the bride's friends volunteered flimsy words of encouragement with no results.

"I need a drink," the bride growled.

Three women shot up and left the room to find

her one.

The next hour was filled with every emotion imaginable. In her drunken stupor, Stephanie would shift suddenly from angry shouted orders, to weeping into a tissue, to laughing maniacally as her friends and family made every attempt to remove the red stains from her dress. When all was said and done, she was left with large, smeared, pink splotches all over what was once a pristine white gown.

"You can hardly see them," her aunt offered.

"Yeah, it kind of looks like that is the style of the dress," a bridesmaid lied.

A knock on the door interrupted what Jen was certain would have been more false praise.

"The limo service is here." Elaine stepped in and placed a tentative hand on her daughter's shoulder.

Pushing her hand away, Stephanie grabbed the beverage sitting next to her, along with the bouquet she had begun to pick apart, and half-stomped, half-stumbled out the door and towards a waiting limo. The driver moved to open the door, but was shoved out of the way by the bride, who flung it ajar, crammed herself inside, and slammed it behind her.

"Well, we can all fit in the other car." Her mother forced a timid laugh.

* * * * *

The ceremony did not go well. It seemed as if the men of the family, who spent the morning enjoying athletic highlights, had also enjoyed some refreshment, and, as Jen imagined, probably indulged in a bit more once the great wine tragedy had occurred.

The entire bridal party appeared sloppy and slow, Stephanie's condition the worst of all. She fidgeted constantly as the minister led them through the ceremony: first lifting and dropping the train of her dress, and then perpetually leaning from one foot to the other, lobbing her head forward and backward in boredom, mouth hanging open as she from time to time flailed her arms about, her bouquet falling to pieces with each hit of the blooms against her leg.

When the ceremony concluded and the bridal party couples made their way back down the aisle, Jen took as many consecutive shots as she could, hoping that at least one of them would be useable.

"I love you, so much," Stephanie slurred, as she hung in the arms of her husband.

"Me, too. Now let's party." He punched a fist in the air.

Well, at least the mood has improved. Jen, already feeling exhausted, watched as the group got into the limos and left for the Ivy Manor.

* * * * *

Seeing as how the party actually began around eight that morning, it didn't take much to get the guests going that night. From the second the bridal party walked into the grand ballroom, the hall filled with raucous celebrating. When Big Al had finished calling the last of the names during the grand entrance, and Jen had snapped the last picture of them, she made her way to the staff table, eager for some sane and sober company.

"Hey, guys," she called over the music.

"Hi, you," Al greeted her.

From the corner of her eye, Jen saw Nate chuckle as Al squished her in a bear hug and then plopped her down in front of the sound mixer.

"How was your cruise?" Jen inquired when he released her.

"Fantastic. Jen, if you can ever take that trip, you've got to. Carol and I had the time of our lives. The food! Oh, I thought my brother could cook..."

"Hi," Nate whispered in her ear, putting his hand on Jen's arm as he walked by her to adjust the volume of the song.

The voice of a groomsman broke into Jen and Al's conversation.

"Hey DJ guy," he called, "could you play that song?"

"Which song?" Nate looked amused.

"You know that one, with the clapping."

"Sure," Nate agreed. "Give me a minute."

Sure enough, a moment later Nate had faded out the previous song, and a popular group dance number took its place.

"Yeah." The partier cheered.

"How could you possibly have known what he was talking about?" Jen laughed.

"Lucky guess," he chuckled.

"Al, I'd love to hear more," she stopped his continued description of the cruise, "but I should get more pictures before it's too late."

"Oh, go...go. Don't want to keep you." He waved her away. "We can talk later."

"See you guys in a bit."

The guests continued to become more rowdy as the night wore on. Few people sat to eat their meals. Instead, they grabbed bites between dances and drinks. Regardless of what song came on, the dance floor was always full, and so was the line at the bar. Jen saw Matty only from a distance, serving up drink after drink and doing shots with the guests.

Unfortunately for Jen, Al, and Nate, the nature of the evening kept them busy and on their feet the entire time. They stopped for only a few seconds here and there when they could get to the table for a bite of dinner, most of which Angie ended up packing for them to take home.

By the time nine o'clock rolled around, guests were in rare form. At a typical reception, Jen found this time the best for celebration-type pictures. People were relaxed and happy. The same couldn't be said, though, on this occasion. Several men and women were slumped down over chairs, or being held up by the shoulder of a friend. Upon seeing yet another inebriated person slip on the dance floor, Jen decided it was time to check in with the bride and groom and call it a night.

"Is there anything else you'd like photos of?" Jen asked the groom when she found him.

"No. We're good."

"All right, I'm all set then. I'll give you a call when I have your proofs."

The groom had already dismissed her and had returned to the conversation with his buddies.

When she reached the DJ stand, Al was going over a list of songs with the bride's mother.

"I'm going to take off," she yelled over the music to Nate, collecting her things as she did. "I'll see you next weekend."

"Actually," Nate picked a bag up off the floor and handed it to her, "Al gave me next weekend off, so I'll see you in two weeks."

"Cool. Enjoy your free weekend."

"Thanks. I will."

"Bye."

"See ya." He waved.

CHAPTER ELEVEN

Jen awoke the next morning earlier than usual, and without the assistance of her alarm. She rolled over, sinking her face into a cool spot on her feather pillow, and loosened the comforter that wrapped tightly around her. The ringing in her ears had faded overnight, as had some of the ache in her muscles. Looking at the clock and discovering the pleasant surprise that it was only a few minutes after six, she stretched leisurely and relaxed a little longer, allowing her body to catch up with how awake her mind was.

That was quite a day. She thought back to the wedding.

Between all of the drama, the physical act of working, and eating dinner in bed, as evidenced by the to-go container balancing precariously on the edge of her nightstand, it was no wonder she fell asleep so quickly and slept so soundly.

She climbed out from under her covers and slipped on an oversized pair of socks. Jen tiptoed into the living room, sat on the couch, picked up the remote, and considered how she'd spend her day as she flipped through the channels.

Today feels like a waffle kind of day. As soon as I hear Claire waking up, I'll mix up a batter, and we can make some for breakfast.

Knowing that wouldn't be for a while, she settled on an infomercial for some type of kitchen chopper and let herself get sucked in.

A loud knock on the door jolted Jen out of her daze.

Frightened, upon realizing how early it was—not even 7:00 a.m.—she froze in her seat. Then cautiously, she stood up and crept towards the door, wondering who could be coming by, uninvited, so early in the day. In the few seconds it took her to reach the entrance, a million scenarios ran through her mind, all of them unpleasant.

Standing on her toes, she looked through the peephole.

"Matty?" she exclaimed, louder than she meant to. Dropping back down onto her heels, she let out a sigh.

She unlocked the door and opened it, the smell of alcohol instantly hitting her in the face.

"Hey, Gorgeous." Matty attempted to reach out and put his hand on her shoulder, before leaning in to kiss her.

"Eww. Matty!" Jen half shouted, half whispered,

as she pushed him hard in the chest with both of her hands. "What's wrong with you? You're completely trashed." Looking at him, she realized he was still in his work clothes from the night before. "Have you been out all night?" She looked at him, disgusted. "How did you even get in the building?"

"Door's open." He waved drunkenly in the general direction of the front door. "You should have stayed. It was a real party." His words slurred together.

"As appealing as you make that sound," she winced at his appearance. "I'm glad I didn't. What are you doing here, anyway?" She was getting annoyed.

"I wanted to see you." His words came out slowly, as if his mouth was having trouble keeping up with his brain, or vice versa. He reached out again, this time grabbing her waist.

A second time she pushed him away, now more aware than before that she was still in her pajamas.

"Go home, Matty." Roughly she removed his hands from the door frame so she could close it.

"Oh fine." He made an attempt to wave his hand at her in dismissal, before turning and stumbling towards the elevator.

"Wait." Jen's voice stopped him. "How did you get here?"

"Drove."

"Ugh." She groaned, her conscience beating out

her disgust for the man that stood in her hallway. "Get in here. You're not driving until you sober up."

She opened the door and motioned towards the couch.

"Sit, and don't make any noise. I'm going to get dressed." She shook her head in repugnance.

Matty did as he was told, and dropped down into the center of the couch, as Jen headed towards her bedroom to change.

Once in her room, she moved fast to get ready. She wanted Matty out of there, and as soon as possible. Grabbing a pair of jeans from the floor, she put them on, along with a tank top and hoodie. Stopping in the bathroom, she quickly brushed her teeth and combed the tangles from her fair hair before pulling it into a ponytail with an elastic band from the dish on the counter.

When she emerged, though it had only been a matter of minutes, she found Matty asleep on the couch.

"Oh, you have *got* to be kidding me," she muttered.

Taking a marker from the junk drawer and the pad of paper from the phone table, Jen scribbled a note to Claire:

Everything's all right.
Went out for a bit.
Be home soon.

— *J*

Jen tore the note off the pad and placed it on the counter, before making her way over to the couch.

"Wake up." She gave Matty a hard shake followed by a slap on the arm.

After a few attempts, he awoke.

"Get up," She snapped.

As he did, Jen took her keys and purse from the table near the door, then stood tapping her foot impatiently as she waited for him to exit. Once they were both in the hallway, she locked the apartment behind her, and, seeing that Matty was in no condition to take the stairs, pressed the down button on the elevator.

"Where we going?"

"Somewhere to sober you up," she answered, not giving him the courtesy of looking at him as they rode down together.

The elevator dinged and the door opened. Both of them got out and left the building. Matty headed for his car.

"I don't think so." She grabbed his arm and pulled him the opposite direction. "We're walking."

Jen, not aware of how much time had passed, realized as they walked that they were no longer the only ones awake in the neighborhood. Several cars were on the road, and employees of the grocery store across the street were opening for the day.

She stopped abruptly at the crosswalk and stuck her arm out in front of Matty, forcing him to come to a halt. When the sign flashed "walk," she crossed the street and paused there just long enough to ensure Matty was still in tow before finishing the walk towards the plaza.

Reaching the door to Java Jane's, she opened it and let Matty in behind her. Then, after instructing him to sit down somewhere, she went to the counter and ordered the largest and strongest black coffee they had to offer that morning.

"Rough night?" The familiar barista asked, tilting her head towards Matty.

"Not for me, but apparently it was for my friend here," Jen answered, trying not to take her annoyance for Matty out on the girl behind the counter. "Thanks." She dropped a dollar in the tip mug when the employee returned with the freshly poured, to-go cup of coffee.

Jen plunked the cup down on the table in front of Matty, splashing a little from the hole in the lid, then took the seat across from him facing the door.

"Drink up. Then I'm taking you home."

They sat in silence, Jen with her arms crossed tightly in front of her, trying to signify to Matty her anger at his early morning visit.

The bell on the door announced the arrival of another customer. Jen lifted her gaze at the sound.

"Nate?" she found herself saying aloud upon seeing him enter the coffee house.

His head turned at the sound of his name. A happy expression that showed his white teeth spread across his face when he saw her across the room.

He was wearing a pair of distressed jeans and a casual, slightly worn, plaid button-up over a t-shirt, the sleeves rolled part way up. He looked different, and it occurred to Jen that this was the first time she had seen him in anything other than work clothes. *He looks...nice.* His dark brown, wavy hair, which he usually combed neatly, was a little disheveled in an intentional kind of way.

"Hey," he called across the coffee house, and strolled towards her.

Suddenly, realizing how it must look — her a total mess, Matty in his clothes from the night before, and the two of them together first thing in the morning — Jen's heart dropped into her stomach as Nate approached her.

"Hey, Man," Matty said louder than necessary, when Nate reached the table.

As if he had just realized the presence of another person, Nate looked down and took notice of Matty.

"How's it goin'?" He stuck out his hand for Matty to shake.

Nate's eyes moved back to Jen. He looked amused.

"So, what are you two up to?" His tone was casual.

"Oh...we're...we're not up to anything." Jen felt panicked. "I mean we're not here together. I mean, we are, but...it's just that Matty...he...showed up and..."

She was flustered, and although she was well aware of her wild gestures, sudden inability to form sentences, and the speed at which words poured out of her mouth, she felt powerless to do anything about it.

Why am I so nervous? Why can't I just explain myself? Why... She stopped to look at Nate. *Why does he just keep smiling at me?*

"What?" Her voice came out in a more demanding and defensive way than she intended.

Nate chuckled.

"You're just funny when you get all worked up."

"Oh," was all Jen could say, as she relaxed slightly and sunk down a bit in her chair, a little embarrassed.

After what felt like an eternity of silence, Jen blurted out the first thing she could think to say. "So, what are you doing here?"

"I'm headed to my sister's to help John put up a fence around their yard. This place was good, so I just figured I'd pick up some breakfast for all of us."

"That's really nice of you," Jen muttered.

For a few moments no one spoke a word. Matty sat drinking his coffee and Nate and Jen remained silent.

"Well, I guess I'm going to order now," Nate stated pleasantly. "I'll see you two around."

"See ya," Matty answered.

"Bye." Jen tried unsuccessfully to catch his eye before he walked away.

"All right, let's get going." Jen looked to Matty.

After allowing him to sip a little more coffee, Jen walked him back to her apartment, where she told him to get into her car, while she, not wanting to be alone with him, went upstairs to get Claire.

"Hi," Jen called, when she opened the door.

Claire was in the kitchen, wrapped in a bathrobe and about to pour herself a bowl of cereal.

"Hey, Hon. Where were you?"

"Could you throw some clothes on and come with me?" Jen let out an exhausted and disgusted sigh.

"Sure. You okay?" Claire suddenly stopped pouring and looked nervously at her best friend.

"Oh, yeah," she reassured her.

Jen told her roommate all about their unwanted guest and the events of the morning, as Claire changed out of her pajamas.

"Ugh, he's awful," Claire announced, after hearing the tale. "I can't believe I ever thought he was good looking," she added as they approached Jen's car.

Claire began yelling at Matty the instant she laid eyes on him.

"You're lucky it was Jen that answered the door this morning and not me, pal." She continued on, barely stopping for breath until they reached his house.

"Get out," she snapped, as soon as the car came to a halt.

A now silent Matty did as Claire had commanded, slamming the car door behind him.

"Wow, what a morning." Claire was immediately calm. Jen backed the car out of the driveway and commenced the ride home. "You seem beat," she added.

"Yeah, kind of. Thanks for coming with me. It was better with you here."

"Sure thing, Sweetie."

The rest of the drive home, the girls sat quietly side by side.

Jen thought about her encounter with Nate that morning. *He sure didn't seem bothered to see me sitting with Matty.* Somehow the thought disappointed her. *What am I doing? Why do I even care? I'm not interested in Nate. I don't sit around daydreaming about him or anything. I don't feel anything for him romantically. When we're together, I don't even think to flirt with him; he's just too much the friend type. I wasn't acting crazy because he walked in,* she tried to explain her actions that morning away. *Had it been anyone else, I would have had the same reaction. It was just that I was there with Matty, first thing in the morning, and I wouldn't want anyone to think I was the kind of person to be with someone like him. That's all it was. Plus, he clearly isn't interested.*

CHAPTER TWELVE

The following week sped by for Jen. As the photos from previous Saturday's drama-filled wedding required a lot more attention than usual, most of her hours were spent in front of her computer, editing. This weekend she hoped would be different.

While the ceremony and reception elements for that day's wedding were typical, the size of the bridal party was not. Looking down at her paperwork, Jen counted the names of over twenty friends of the bride and groom that would be participating in the day with them.

Well, at least I'll have an abundance of pictures to choose from.

The apartment was quiet that morning as she packed up the food and equipment needed for the day. Claire had left before Jen even awoke, to get some extra hours in at the lab before her date that evening. And so Jen was left with plenty of time alone to contemplate how she would go about getting all the pictures she needed that day.

Deciding that she should get all the still life, flower, and church building shots out of the way prior to the bridal party's arrival, she packed up her car and left early.

Traffic was slow. Jen drove over a large area of road under construction. The overwhelming stench of blacktop hung in the air as men filled and smoothed potholes and cracks in the street, caused by the expansion of freezing water over the course of the past winter. Just as the end of the orange barrels were in sight, Jen's right front tire fell hard into a pothole too large to avoid, the rear tire right behind it.

"Oh, great," she exclaimed, as something underneath her rattled noisily.

The car was loud, and the rattling was becoming more intense with every yard she drove. Suddenly, Jen heard a loud clunk, followed by a scraping, as if something were being dragged behind her.

She managed to pull into the next driveway, a shopping center parking lot. Jen stopped her car in the first space she saw. Shutting off the engine, she got out to look at the damage, then, trying her best to stay clean, got on her hands and knees to check underneath the car.

While Jen in no way considered herself a mechanical expert, she did know that dragging what appeared to be her exhaust system along the ground wasn't good.

What am I going to do? She looked at her watch, already beginning to worry about the time. *I need a car today, or at least a way to get to the church.* She paused to think. *I'll call my parents,* she decided. Then, pulling her phone from her purse and opening it, she remembered that they were out of town, and closed it once again.

Claire's at work.

She remembered her conversation with Nate the previous weekend. *He's off today.*

Reopening her phone, she scrolled down to Smith, Nate, and pressed the green call button.

After one ring, she heard his voice on the other end of the phone.

"Hello?"

"Hey, Nate. This is Jen."

"Hey, Jen. What's going on?" he answered cheerfully.

"I'm sorry to bug you on your Saturday off, but I was wondering if I could ask you a huge favor." She leaned against her out-of-commission vehicle.

"Anything. Are you all right?" His voice was noticeably concerned.

"I'm fine, it's just that, my car broke down, and I'm on my way to a wedding. I was wondering if you could give me a ride to the church?"

"Of course. Where are you right now?"

"I'm at the Stop 'N' Save on Rt. 203."

"All right, let me get changed, and I'll be there in about 15 minutes."

"Oh, thank you so much. You're a total life saver."

"It's no problem. I'll see you in a few. Bye."

"Bye."

Jen breathed a sigh of relief as she closed her phone. Checking the time, she was glad she'd left as early as she had.

A quarter of an hour later, Jen saw Nate's forest green SUV pulling into the supermarket parking lot. She gave him a wave to get his attention.

"Hi." He stepped out of the vehicle, wearing his usual work tux.

"Hi. Thank you so much for helping me. I don't know what I'd do if you weren't here."

"Well, don't thank me yet. I haven't gotten you where you need to go. Let's get your stuff." He opened the back of his SUV and helped Jen transfer her belongings from one trunk to the other.

"Hop in." He closed up the back and opened the passenger side door for her.

"I thought you weren't working today," Jen said when he got in the driver's side next to her. "Why are you in your tux?"

"Well, if I'm driving you around all day, I can't very well be standing around a wedding in jeans and a t-shirt, can I?" He glanced over at her, looking pleased with himself. "So where are we headed?"

"St. Joseph's on River Street," she answered. "That's thoughtful, but I don't want to take up your whole day."

"How else are you going to get around? Plus, it'll be fun. I never get to see this side of a wedding. Maybe I'll get to experience a crazy aunt or two," he joked.

Jen was touched.

"Thank you. This is so nice of you."

"Don't worry about it." He tapped her with his elbow, making light of the huge service he was doing her.

They sat for a moment without saying anything, and Jen's mind returned to the thing it had so often over the past week: their unexpected meeting on Sunday.

"Nate?"

"Yeah?"

"About last Sunday..." Jen began. "I know I was acting kind of crazy, but I just wanted to let you know that there is nothing going on with me and Matty."

Nate said nothing and let her continue.

"He showed up at my apartment that morning. Apparently, he had been partying at the Manor all night. I didn't want him driving, so I took him to get some coffee before Claire and I drove him home."

"I was wondering how you both ended up there."

"You were?"

"Yeah, but for the record, I knew you two weren't together."

"You did?"

"Of course." He gave a little laugh.

"But...how?" Jen felt confused.

"Well for one, at weddings I see how he looks at you, and how you look at him, or rather, that you don't. Plus, last week we had just spent like an hour talking about relationships, and clearly he isn't what you said you wanted." Nate paused. "So...tell me," he continued, "how will I be helping you today?"

"You don't need to..." Jen trailed off. Her mouth was answering his question, but her mind was still concentrating on the rush of relief she felt upon hearing that Nate knew Matty was not her type.

"Don't argue," he teased. "If you don't tell me how I can help, I'll just make stuff up on my own, and who knows how that will go." His good-natured reply lightened the mood.

"Well, I certainly don't want that," she joked, already feeling more at ease. "How about we unload the car," she suggested, as they pulled into the nearly empty church lot.

"That, I can do."

Jen pointed to each bag she would need, and Nate, picking up every one, carried them all inside for her and placed them, per her instruction, on the back pew in the sanctuary.

"What do you do now?"

"Usually, I pick up a program and go over what's going to happen and when, and I take any left over time to get pictures of flowers and things."

"Why don't you get the photos you need, and I'll find you a program?"

"That'd be great. Thanks."

They each went their separate ways to do their respective jobs. When Jen had finished getting the shots she needed both outdoors and in, she returned to find Nate sitting in the pew next to her things, looking over the program that he had picked up.

"Here you go." He handed her the paper as she sat down next to him.

"Thanks." She leaned in to look it over.

"So, now do you plan the pictures you'll be taking?" He sounded genuinely interested.

"Sort of. I know I need a picture of every major moment." She pointed to the items on the program. "Since I usually stop by the rehearsal the night before, I know how long each part takes. Now, I just review the plan I made in my head last night, of where I want to be shooting from for each part of the ceremony." After a period of walking through the steps, her eyes were drawn to the front door. "Looks like the bridal party is arriving."

"What can I do?" Nate stood up.

"Well, when bridal parties are huge like this,

things can get disorganized. Could you let people know where to go when they come in? The groomsmen and the groom's family head down that hall to the library." She pointed the way. "The bridesmaids and bride's family go into the bridal room right there." She pointed again.

"Sure thing."

"Great. Thanks. I'll be taking pictures with the bride and her friends first; then I'll do pictures of the men. See you in a bit."

Pictures of the bride and her bridesmaids went well. Spirits were high, and Jen used the large number of women constantly moving in and out of the dressing room to her advantage, getting a variety of different shots. Knowing they would be going to the park after the ceremony and would have plenty of time for photos, she saved most of the posed concepts for later.

Once the bride was dressed, Jen snapped a last image of her with her friends getting ready, then left them to relax so she could take photos of the groom and his bunch.

"How'd it go in there?" Nate asked when he saw Jen come out of the dressing room.

"Good. You?"

"Everything was fine out here. An aunt did come in, though." He laughed.

"Uh oh. Trouble?"

"No. She just wanted to know where to take the boutonnieres. I told her the library. I hope that was right."

"It was. I'm headed there now. Do you wanna come? I mean, if you don't, that's fine..." Jen stopped, realizing how boring a task that might seem to him.

"Yeah. This is like secret insider kind of stuff."

They walked together to the library. Jen knocked on the open door to indicate her presence. The groom and his family welcomed her in.

"Hi. I'm Jen." She introduced herself to the group as a whole, as she had not yet met all of them. "This is Nate. We'll be with you all day doing the photography."

Once the introductions were completed, Jen organized some of the classic photos: the groom with his Mom, putting on the boutonniere, he with his best man standing together talking, and then a few candid shots similar to those of the bride and her friends.

Nate stood off to the side, helping the groom's mother pass out flowers.

After taking her last picture, Jen addressed the groom. "Well, it's just about time for the ceremony to get underway, so we'll see you in there."

* * * * *

When the ceremony had concluded and the last of the long line of attendants had finished their walk down the aisle, Jen met Nate in the back of the sanctuary. Together they packed up her equipment, and again Nate did all the heavy lifting, making the trip to the car much easier than it usually would have been.

"I could get used to this," Jen declared as he put the last of her things in back.

"Yeah. Hanging out with you all day isn't half as bad as I thought it would be," he joked.

"You're rotten." She gave his arm a little whack, and then reached to the backseat to retrieve her grocery bag. "Want a snack?" she offered.

"Sure. That sounds good."

Jen opened two sports drinks and put one in Nate's cup holder, the other in her own. Then she handed him a granola bar and some beef jerky.

"Do you always bring this with you?" He laughed.

"Yes. They go good together. You'll see."

Jen gave Nate the last instruction of where to turn, just as they finished their food.

"I admit, that was a better combination than I expected," Nate confessed when they pulled into a spot near the limos. "So, what do we need out of the car for this location?" He moved the gearshift into park.

"Just my camera and that flat round case."

Together they left the SUV and entered the park, Nate carrying what appeared to be a giant black dot.

"Could you hand me that?" Jen pointed to the round case, after having posed the bride and groom seated underneath a tree.

"Sure."

Jen unzipped the case and removed a gold and white circle that seemed to spring into life upon being released from its container, tripling in size as it did so.

"Whoa. Wasn't expecting that." Nate appeared amazed.

"Nobody ever does," Jen laughed. "Would you mind standing to the right of them and holding this overhead to block the sunlight?"

"Sure." He took the reflector from her. "Here?" He positioned the circle between himself and the couple, blocking the sun's bright rays.

"Yes, perfect." She turned her attention to the bride and groom. "All right, one, two, three."

Jen pressed the shutter button, and the happy couple smiled at her. Nate peeked under the reflector, trying to get an idea of what Jen was seeing.

As a group, they moved through the park, stopping here and there for pictures. First, they were posed in a field, where the bridesmaids sat surrounding the bride. Nate, following Jen's instructions, held the reflector to shine a golden light on the group of friends. Near the field, along the tree line, were a group of picnic tables, one of which Jen used in a photograph as a way to stagger the heights of the groom and his groomsmen, with some of them standing, some sitting on a bench, and others on the table itself. Next, the entire party stretched across a low bridge that spanned a small pond. Then, Jen, struck with an artistic whim, worked with the bride and groom to photograph them as a gentle breeze blew along the water, causing the bride's veil and dress to be swept delicately through the air as the couple kissed at the water's edge. All the while she felt Nate's eyes on her.

"You're amazing," Nate whispered, as he and Jen walked ahead of the bridal party to the next destination.

"What?" Jen stopped.

"As a photographer." He quickly clarified what he meant. "The way you see things, or maybe it's the way you set things up, I don't know. It's just, when I look at what you're taking a picture of. I see this...thing, like a moment that I wouldn't have seen otherwise. Like I'm seeing a significant time in that person's life. I guess I'm not explaining this very well. Sorry."

"No. Thank you." Jen kept her eyes on him as they walked. "That means a lot."

"I don't see how," Nate laughed. "I'm not even making any sense."

"Trust me when I say that when it comes to artistic things, those are the best kind of compliments. Honestly, I know my job is to document each couple's big day, but deep down, I always want to take the kind of pictures that make people feel something, something you can't describe.

"Well you do."

"Thanks."

"So, where to now?"

"Let's take one last stop, over by those fountains. The bride wanted a photo with each of her bridesmaids."

* * * * *

Once finished in the park, Nate's SUV joined the caravan of limos driving toward the Ivy Manor.

The grand ballroom was packed with guests, far more so than the church was earlier that day. Nate and Jen wound their way through the tables and invitees to the DJ stand, where Nate met Al to explain his presence that evening.

"Hi, Uncle," Jen overheard him say as he approached Al.

"I thought I gave you the night off. What are you doing here?" Al looked surprised.

"Jen was having car trouble this morning, so I've been driving her around. I'll be here all night, so if you need anything, let me know."

"That's my nephew." Al beamed proudly. "Always coming to someone's rescue." He patted Nate on the back. "I'll have Frankie make up an extra plate for you."

"Thanks. That'd be great."

* * * * *

That evening the bride and groom had selected to include not only some of the typical reception events, but rather, all of them. Once they made their grand entrance, the couple enjoyed their first dance together. Jen stood on the sidelines, capturing the pair as they glided around the dance floor, appearing to have taken lessons together in preparation for the event. Shortly after, their bridal party joined them for another dance. Prior to the plates of prime rib and roasted chicken being served, the bride and groom cut their cake.

Jen, along with a number of other guests, surrounded the table and waited with baited breath to see what they would do.

"I'm thinking they are going to smash it," Nate whispered in Jen's ear.

"Oh, for sure."

They each lifted a larger than normal piece off of the plate, then, looking at each other, held it in mid-air before mischievously aiming for each other's faces, trying in the process to avoid the square of frosting-covered goodness headed towards their own.

The crowd laughed and clapped along with the bride and groom as the pair wiped frosting off each other's cheeks and licked the icing off their fingers. Jen pressed the shutter down as Nate whispered from behind her again.

"That was a pretty good one."

"Definitely." She nodded.

* * * * *

When the guests consumed all there was to eat, the dancing got underway. Al was in excellent form, alternating between special events, slow love songs, and crowd pleasing 60's favorites, keeping the happy-go-lucky throng content all night.

Finally, near ten-thirty, guests began to make their exits, allowing Jen to pack up for the evening.

Together, she and Nate left the Ivy Manor, heading towards his SUV. After securing all of her equipment in the back, Nate removed his tux jacket and threw it in the backseat before getting in and starting the car.

"I can't thank you enough," Jen began as soon as they sat in the quiet of the vehicle together.

"It was fun," Nate assured her. He rolled up the sleeves of his white dress shirt before moving the gearshift into drive and heading out towards her apartment.

"You were such a huge help, and not just by driving. Everything you did. You have no idea how much easier that made things for me today. How can I repay you?"

"There's no need. I'm happy to help."

"I have to do something." Jen paused. "I know."

150

She snapped her fingers. "How about if I take some pictures of Ruby?"

Nate sat quiet for a minute.

"Please?" Jen pleaded.

"Well..."

"Great!" Jen jumped at the first sign of acceptance, not letting him finish.

"You don't even know what I was going to say," Nate laughed.

"Okay, what were you going to say?"

"I'm going to my sister's house next Sunday afternoon, just to hang out and have a BBQ; you could come with me, and if the mood strikes you, you could take some pictures there, but only if you want to."

"I'd love to," Jen agreed whole-heartedly.

"Cool."

Jen directed Nate to the apartment building across the street from Java Jane's, where he parked in a space near the door before shutting off the car and getting out to open the back. Carrying all of her things, they entered the building and ascended the first flight of stairs.

"I am such an idiot," Jen exclaimed, stopping on the first landing.

"What?" Nate stopped alongside her.

"I'm sorry. Here you are carrying all my junk, and I make you take the stairs. It's force of habit, I guess."

Nate began walking again, grinning as he did so.

"It's not going to kill me to walk up a few steps," he joked. "You always take the stairs?"

"Yep." Jen felt glad that he didn't mind the climb, despite the heavy load he was carrying, and caught up to him as she spoke. "I figure I've got legs, so I might as well use them while I can."

"I can appreciate that. So what floor are we stopping on?"

"Six. When your legs hurt you know you have one more floor to go," she added.

"Well, then, we should have stopped three floors ago," he kidded.

They reached the sixth floor and Jen turned down the hallway towards her door. Nate waited as she pulled out her keys and unlocked it.

"Claire, are you home?" She called into the apartment.

"In the kitchen," answered Claire.

"Come on in." Jen held the door open for Nate.

"Claire, this is Nate. Nate, Claire." She introduced them when her roommate came walking into the living room.

"It's so nice to finally meet you." Claire tried and failed to hide her suspicious grin.

"You, too," Nate replied, moving into the room to shake her hand, still carrying all of Jen's camera equipment. "I've heard so much about you."

"Oh, I'm sorry." Jen starting removing things from

his shoulders. "You can put all of that down. I'll just throw it in my room." She collected what she could.

"Thanks." He handed her the last of the bags.

"Well, I'm gonna get going," Nate announced, jabbing a thumb towards the door, when Jen re-entered the room.

"Thank you, again, so much." Jen walked with him towards the exit.

"It was fun."

From the corner of her eye, Jen watched Claire pretending to be preoccupied in the kitchen.

"So, I'll give you a call this week with the details for Sunday."

"Sounds great." She felt suddenly nervous.

"All right." Nate paused. "Good night." He opened the door. "It was nice to meet you, Claire." He waved towards the kitchen.

"Oh, you, too," she called back over the clattering of pots, peaking her head around the cupboards.

"Good night," he said again, looking Jen in the eyes.

"Night," Jen replied quietly, before he turned out the door and walked towards the stairs.

CHAPTER THIRTEEN

That Sunday during church, Jen couldn't keep her mind on what was going on around her. Whether it was the idea of spending the day with Nate that had her so antsy, or the sure signs of summer, she wasn't sure, but considering the magnificent May day she had awoken to, she decided on the latter.

The sun was warm and shining, and the clear blue sky was full of billowy white clouds. *The perfect day to be outside enjoying a BBQ,* she thought as she traveled back home.

Once inside, she had only a few minutes until Nate would be there to pick her up. Sure enough, the buzzer rang right on time.

"Claire, could you buzz him up?" Jen called from her room.

"'Course."

"Hello?" Claire spoke into the intercom.

"Hi. It's Nate."

"Come on in." Claire held the button to unlock the door downstairs for him.

Jen stood in her room giving herself one more look over in the full-length mirror. After much deliberation earlier that day on what to wear, she had decided on a pair of jeans, a brightly colored graphic T, and her favorite pair of red sneakers. Her hair was loose except for the small front braid she had just finished. She felt comfortable.

A knock on the door came just as Jen was leaving her room.

"Hi, Nate." Jen saw Claire welcome him when she opened the door.

"Hi, Claire. Good to see you again," he greeted her cheerfully.

"Come on in."

Nate entered the apartment and Jen met his grin as she came down the hall.

He looked much as he had the day she saw him at Java Jane's. His jeans, T-shirt, and somewhat disheveled hair matched Jen's casual look.

"Hi. You ready to go?"

"Yep. I just gotta grab these, and my camera." Jen stepped into the kitchen and unplugged the crock-pot that had been warming the baked beans she told Nate she would bring.

"Here, let me help."

Nate wrapped the cord around the small appliance and carried it to the door. Jen slung her purse and camera bag over her shoulder before saying goodbye to Claire.

"Have a good day."

"You too, Girlie. Have fun, you two," Claire called.

"We will. Bye," Nate added. "Let's go." Nate turned the opposite direction of the elevator, and headed directly towards the stairs.

"I've really been looking forward to this," Jen commented.

"Me, too. I think you and my family will get along great."

"I hope so. I can't wait to meet them."

The journey to his sister's home was a little bit of a trek, but an enjoyable one.

"I love coming out to the country." Nate rolled down the window and let the sweet spring breeze fill the SUV as he zoomed up and over hills along the country roads.

"This is beautiful." Jen enjoyed the scenery as it flashed past.

As they whizzed by field after open field, each house further from the last, Jen and Nate shared conversation that was light and easy, first about Jen's car repair, then work, and finally about different television shows they had both been watching.

"We're almost there." Nate decreased his speed as they neared town and began to travel around the city square.

"What a great place."

"Yeah, my sister loves it here. She says there's just enough civilization. Ruby has a big yard to play in, and the square is so close that Susan can take walks over here with her all the time."

"How fun. I wonder if that ice cream place is any good." Jen pointed as they passed a small parlor on the third street of the square.

"We'll have to try it when they open up for the summer. I've never been, but Suz says Ruby is crazy for the kids' cones over there." Nate pulled into a driveway. "Here we are."

Susan's house was just as Jen had pictured. The small white home sat on a large yard of freshly cut grass. Well-manicured but simple flowerbeds lined the front, and a white picket fence surrounded the back yard and its tall oak trees.

"This is perfect."

"Isn't it?" Nate grinned, then got out and opened Jen's car door, before retrieving the crock-pot from the back. "Come on. I want you to meet everyone!"

"Uncle Nate!" Ruby cried as she came running out the back door towards him.

Nate lifted the pot just in time, as Ruby threw her small arms around his legs in the biggest embrace possible for such a tiny person.

"There's my Rubester," Nate greeted her.

Crouching down, he set the appliance on the

ground and returned the hug.

Jen happily watched the exchange between her friend and his adorable niece.

"Hold me. Hold me," she begged, jumping up and down as Nate stood up again with the baked beans.

Nate's brother-in-law approached. "Give him a second, Rube."

He too was just as Jen had pictured: tall and lean, with had dark hair that was just starting to gray at the temples.

"Hey, John. This is my friend Jen."

Jen extended her hand. "Hi. It's nice to meet you."

"Same here." He grinned as he shook her hand. "Here, let me take that." John patted Nate's shoulder, then relieved him of the pot he was carrying. "Come on in."

Ruby jumped up and down, her hands reaching up to Nate, her short brown bob bouncing with every hop.

"Now I can hold you." Nate playfully picked her up and spun her around. After a few circles, he turned her around to face Jen. "Ruby, this is Miss Jen."

"Hi, Ruby." Jen gave her a little wave.

"She has pretty hair," Ruby commented to Nate after looking Jen over.

"Yes she does," Nate agreed.

"Do you want to see my princesses?" Ruby inquired of Jen.

"I'd love to."

"How quickly I'm replaced," Nate joked as Ruby struggled to get down and then ran into the house ahead of them.

Nate, Jen, and John followed her through the back door.

"Hi, Suz." Nate leaned in to give her a kiss on the cheek as she worked at the kitchen counter. "This is Jen. Jen, this is my sister Susan."

"Great to meet you." Susan stopped her work to give Jen a hug.

"You, too." Jen looked around, admiring the charming decorations. "Your house is lovely."

"Thanks. We like it."

"Is there anything I can do to help?"

"Actually, I think we're about ready. You and Nate just grab a drink and go relax outside. I'll be out in a minute."

Nate filled two tall glasses with crushed ice and poured ice-cold tea from a pitcher, then, taking two lemon circles from a dish in the fridge, dropped one inside each glass. All the while, Ruby, who had pulled Jen to the floor, was displaying and naming each of her princess toys, one by one.

"Here you go." Nate handed the glass down to Jen.

"Thanks."

"Ruby, what do you want to drink?" He looked to

his niece.

"Pink milk."

Taking one of the many sippy cups from the cupboard, Nate filled it with milk, then added two scoops of strawberry powder before attaching the lid and shaking it up.

"There you go. You ladies ready to go outside?"

"Sure," Jen answered.

Nate held out his free hand to help Jen up. Ruby, after carefully considering which of her princesses she wanted to play with, selected three, and ran for the door, sippy cup tucked under her arm.

"So is this the fence you put up the other weekend?" Jen motioned towards the white enclosure that surrounded the back yard.

"Yep."

"It took a couple of days, but I think it looks pretty good," John added as they joined him on the stone patio.

The outdoor entertaining area was home to a propane grill, and a comfortable patio furniture set that surrounded a granite fire pit.

Jen took a seat on the loveseat and placed her drink on the table portion of the fire pit in front of her. Nate sat down next to her and did the same.

"Perfect day for the first BBQ of the season, isn't it?" John sighed contentedly.

"Sure is," both Nate and Jen agreed.

The trio talked and drank their beverages until Susan came out with a tray full of hamburger patties and marinated chicken.

The smell of grilling meats wafted through the air as they all relaxed, getting to know Jen, and just enjoying each other's company. John occasionally got up to flip a burger or turn the chicken. Laughter spread throughout their conversation, as they watched Ruby jumping and playing pretend in the grass.

"Looks like everything's just about done," John declared from the grill. "Does everyone want cheese on their burgers?"

"Yes, please." The group conceded.

"Ruby, come get some dinner," Susan called into the yard.

"Mom, I want to play."

"We need our Rubester to come eat with us," Nate called back.

"Why do you call her Rubester?"

"Rubester. Like the little boy Rueben in 'Camp Coocoopa'," Nate replied as if the answer were obvious.

"Oh, yeah. I guess...wait, what?" Jen looked at Nate confused.

Nate returned her baffled gaze.

Jen continued. "What's Camp...Coo-coo...whatever?"

"You've *never* seen that movie?" Nate put his hands on her shoulders and turned her towards himself in disbelief.

"I've never even heard of it." Jen shrugged.

"Camp Coo-coo-pa, our home away from home," John began singing an off-key anthem.

"Camp Coo-coo-pa..." Nate stood and joined his brother-in-law in song, each of them placing a hand on their hearts as if reciting a pledge, John still holding a pair of grilling tongs.

"Oh, make it stop," Susan begged. "Neither of them can sing a note to save their lives," she hinted loudly in the men's direction. "They're totally obsessed with that movie. They do this all the time," she added apologetically to Jen.

"Excuse me?" Nate stopped mid-song. "I'm obsessed? Who made me watch that movie every single night, all summer long, when we were in high school?"

"All right, all right, I did," she admitted. "It is pretty funny," she whispered to Jen. "Completely mindless, but funny."

"We should watch it sometime." Nate sat down and tapped Jen's arm with the back of his hand.

"Anything that could make you do that," she waved her hand in the direction where he and John had taken up their song, "I have *got* to see!"

"Enough about weird 70's comedies. Let's eat,"

Susan suggested.

* * * * *

With the exception of the occasional "these beans are delicious" or "this chicken is so moist," the next half hour was filled with a lot less conversation and a lot more chewing. When the meal was finished, Jen helped Susan clean up in the kitchen.

"Thank you for dinner. It was excellent." Jen took the dish Susan had just washed, dried it and placed it with the others in a cupboard.

"We're glad you could come. Nate has been talking a lot about you."

"He has?"

"Yeah, he's been telling us what a great photographer you are."

Jen felt inexplicably let down by her clarification.

"He's just being nice," Jen replied, hoping the disappointment she was feeling hadn't shown. She wanted to change the subject. "Speaking of photography, I don't know if Nate mentioned it, but would it be all right if I took some pictures of Ruby?"

"That'd be wonderful."

Upon finishing the dishes, Susan made a pot of coffee and took, out of the cupboard, a bag of jumbo marshmallows, chocolate bars, and a box of graham crackers, while Jen removed her digital camera from its bag. Together they carried the items along with a tray of coffee mugs, a carafe, and all the necessary coffee additives outside to the patio.

They returned to a warm fire, blazing in the pit in the center of the table. Nate and John were gathering sticks for the marshmallows, and Ruby sat at the edge of the stone patio, playing with a pile of weeds and wildflowers she had picked from the grass.

Jen held one finger to her lips, and then pointed to Ruby to indicate she wanted to get a picture of the moment. Creeping quietly around furniture, Jen knelt down behind the grill and took a few pictures of her friend's niece.

When she stood up, Nate and John, who had been watching what she was doing, came forward with the marshmallow roasting sticks they had found.

Together the four of them sat toasting, and now and then catching fire to and extinguishing, the sugary puffs.

"Rube, do you want a s'more?" John stood up to put his finished marshmallow between two graham crackers.

"Mmm hmm," she answered enthusiastically, getting up from the ground and hopping into the chair her dad had previously occupied.

"Can I have my seat back?" He handed her the dessert.

Ruby shook her head no, and giggled, as she sat holding her s'more with two hands, tapping her toes together, her tiny legs sticking straight out in front of her, not quite reaching the edge of the cushion.

Jen picked up her camera and took a shot of her relishing her dessert, melted chocolate in the corners of her smile.

* * * * *

The rest of the afternoon passed much faster than Jen would have liked. Soon the sun was low and the stars began to make their appearance. Between stopping to take pictures of the cute things Ruby was doing and all the fun the two adult pairs had laughing together, the hours had flown by.

"We should probably get going." Nate turned to Jen when it had grown too dark to see anything outside the ring of light that the fire provided.

"Yeah, I guess we should," she agreed reluctantly.

"Thank you so much for having me." She looked to Susan and John. "It's been wonderful."

"We're glad you could come," they both agreed.

* * * * *

The ride home also went by quickly, and, before long, they had arrived at Jen's building.

Together they climbed the stairs.

"Thank you again for inviting me. I had an amazing time. Your family's so great."

"Thanks for coming, and for taking pictures of Ruby."

"I was happy to." They reached her door. "Well..." Jen's voice trailed off.

Together they stood in the hall, the empty crock-pot in Jen's hands.

"You working this weekend?" Nate quickly filled the silence.

"No. The Manor is booked, but the couple has a different photographer. I've got like a zillion engagement sessions lined up this week, though."

"Oh, well, I hope they go well. I'll see you the next weekend, then?"

"Yep. I'll see you then. Thanks again for today. It was a blast."

"I had fun, too. See ya." He touched her arm fondly, before turning back towards the stairs.

"Bye," she called behind him.

CHAPTER FOURTEEN

The next day, Jen had so much editing work to do that she hardly had a moment to think of anything else. Having slept in later than a typical Monday, she skipped her leisurely getting-ready routine. After pouring and reheating a cup of coffee that Claire had left in the pot for her that morning, Jen sat down at her desk and began her work.

Okay, focus. She tried to tear her eyes away from the gorgeous day taunting her through the window and center them back on her work.

She'd taken more pictures than usual at the wedding with the large bridal party, and had gotten behind on her editing. Even though more than a week had gone by, she had yet to order the proofs. Wanting to get at least one wedding out of the way, she uploaded the finished images to her printer's website and placed the request for over 400 prints before beginning the editing process on her most recent event.

Picture after picture she sharpened and cropped. Skin blemishes were removed and lighting improved, until finally Jen looked at the clock just in time to see it switch from 4:58 to 4:59 p.m.

Finally, she thought, letting out a large sigh and flopping back into her chair after saving the last picture she worked on that day. Still having a few minutes until Claire got home, and wanting to see the photographs she took the previous day with Nate's family, Jen removed the memory card from her camera bag and plugged it into the front of her computer. Flipping through them, she sighed happily, pleased with what she had to work with, and remembering fondly moments of the day before.

"Hiya, Sweetie." Claire's voice interrupted Jen's thoughts.

"Oh, hey." She exited out of the photo viewer. "How was your day?"

"Same old, same old. You?"

"I got a ton done."

"That's good. I'm famished. What about you?"

"Starved." Jen realized how hungry she was upon hearing the mention of food. "I've barely stopped at all today. Would you want to pick something up, so we don't have to wait for anything to cook?"

"My thoughts exactly." Claire was already putting her purse back on her shoulder and heading towards the door. "I'll go get us something. You get the plates and drinks together. Is there anything you have a taste for?"

"Surprise me."

"K. Be back in a few."

Jen put two plates in the oven, set it to warm, and placed two glasses in the freezer to chill while waiting for Claire to return.

Half an hour later, her roommate walked in the door. "Burritos," she sang, holding the bags in the air as she entered the apartment.

"Mmm." Jen's stomach growled.

She pulled a pair of frosty glasses from the freezer, filled them with ice and soda, and then gathered some extra napkins and removed warmed plates from the oven.

"Here's yours." Claire produced a giant foil-wrapped burrito with cryptic markings on the outside. Extra guacamole." She pointed to the writing and placed it on Jen's preheated dish.

"You're the best."

They plopped down on the couch and dove into their tortillas stuffed with chicken, cheese, rice, salsa, and guacamole, enjoying every bite of their spicy Mexican feast.

"So, tell me about yesterday." Claire removed a tray of freshly made tortilla chips from a second bag, placed it on the coffee table, and then, after dipping one into some sour cream, began crunching on it.

"It was such a blast. Nate's family is great. His niece is adorable. I think the pictures I got should be pretty good."

"Can I see them later?"

"'Course," Jen tried to reply with a mouth full of burrito. "They made the best grilled chicken," she continued once she swallowed the large bite. "I meant to ask Susan for the marinade recipe so we could make it."

"Mmm. Can't wait. So what'd you all do?"

"Mostly just talked, joked around, ate, and watched Ruby. It was pretty low key."

"Sounds nice."

"It was. So what'd you do last night?"

"Just bummed around," Claire answered. "Watched TV and looked over some notes for work." She paused. "A guy from the office asked me out today."

"Claire! You should have started with that. Do tell." Jen moved closer to her friend.

"Okay, well..." Claire put her burrito down, and clapped her hands together, matching Jen's excitement. "His name is Emmitt. He's tall, on the thin side, shaves his head, has brown eyes, and always has on a fantastic suit. He's just unbelievably gorgeous." She added extra emphasis to the last two words.

"So when are you two going out?"

"I don't know."

"What do you mean, you don't know?" Jen playfully hit Claire in the leg.

"I told him I'd have to think about it, because we work together and all."

"Oh. That's right, you did say that. Well, I always hear about people who date their co-workers."

"Yeah, me too, and then about what a nightmare it is when they break up."

"Good point," Jen agreed. "So what are you going to do?"

"I'm not sure yet. I *would* like to say yes. We don't work anywhere near the same area. In fact, we only see each other in the cafeteria." She cocked her head to one side thoughtfully. "Ah, what's the worst that could happen? If we go out and then have some awful break-up, I'll just work out at the gym during my lunch hour to avoid him. That way, if we do run into each other, I'll look great and he'll feel bad for ever having let me go," Claire joked.

"That's the spirit. There's nothing like plotting your revenge on a guy you've never dated, for a break-up you've never had," Jen jested.

* * * * *

The rest of both Jen's week and weekend filled with one engagement shoot after another. Between seeing several couples every day and working on all of their pictures, in addition to the images from the last wedding, she couldn't remember all she had ordered when the package that held her proofs arrived at her door the following Wednesday.

171

She always loved this moment. Something about seeing her work in print was such a thrill, regardless of how many times it happened.

Taking a pair of scissors from the junk drawer in the kitchen, she cut the tape along the top of the box, and then did the same with the cellophane that encased her prints in their waxy envelopes. Seeing a picture from the wedding she shot two weeks ago through a foggy envelope, she carefully flipped through the prints to her favorite post cake cutting moment. The happy frosting covered couple in the picture made her smile.

After looking through the stack a second time with a more discerning eye, Jen returned the photos to their envelopes and lifted the next group of prints. Opening it, she saw the picture she had taken of Ruby sitting on the patio with her wildflowers. Jen gathered all the photos from her day with Nate's family and sat down on the couch to look them over. She came across one she had taken of Nate and Ruby together. Jen stopped and gazed at the picture. Ruby sat on Nate's lap. He pretended to be surprised by something Ruby was doing, and the way his mouth was open, and his shoulders were pulled back showed it. Even though Jen made the photograph black and white, she could still see warmness in his eyes, as if it were happening that very instant in front of her.

After looking through the rest of the pictures from the BBQ, Jen placed them back in their envelope and went to retrieve the next set of proofs she had ordered. Setting Nate's down, she looked back and forth between the paper container that held his photos and the pile of engagement proofs she had yet to see. Without any more thought about it, she picked up his photographs and headed towards the door.

Halfway to the Manor, Jen realized, having stopped there earlier in the day, that Nate wasn't at work. *I'll just leave them in his office with a note. That way he can have them sooner. I don't need to be there when he sees them.*

The parking lot of the Ivy Manor was empty. Jen parked right by the door, dashed out of her car, unlocked the large doors, and skipped up the steps. Stopping at Nate's office, she turned the doorknob. *Unlocked. Perfect.*

She switched on the light. Nate's space was neat and organized, much more so than hers. From the top of the desk that sat in the far corner of the room, Jen took a sticky note, and, leaning over, placed a pen to it. Not knowing exactly what to write, she stopped and stood up again.

"Hey." Nate's friendly voice came unexpectedly from the doorway.

"Ah!" Jen screamed, and the pen went flying out of her hand.

Nate laughed.

"What are you doing here?" He shook his head as she scrambled around to find the writing utensil she had dropped.

"I came to bring you this." She turned towards him, and held up the foggy envelope that contained his pictures.

Nate strolled across the room.

"What is it?"

"The pictures of Ruby." Jen was trying her best to contain her excitement as she handed them over.

"Awesome." He spoke with as much elation as Jen was feeling and took them from her hand.

"I hope you like them." She swept her hair to the side and anxiously twisted it.

"I'm sure I will." Nate looked at her, an expression of genuine joy on his face, before returning his gaze to the unopened package.

Quiet fell between them as he removed the photos from their protective sleeve.

"Wow," Nate exclaimed upon seeing the first image of Ruby and her flowers. "Jen..." He paused as he laughed at one of Ruby and John. "These are just amazing!"

Jen stood close to him, looking at each photo as Nate did, interested to see which ones he'd linger on or say something about.

"These are fantastic." When he had reached the

beginning again, he went through the set a second time.

"You like them?"

Nate put the pictures on the desk in front of them, and, once his hands were free, pulled Jen towards him, wrapping his arms around her.

"Yes. Thank you, so much." He hugged her, then slowly relaxed his hold and let her go, still leaving his hands on her upper arms.

"I'm so glad you do. Your family is incredible. I wanted to do a good job."

"They will love these." Nate dropped his hands and picked the pictures back up to look through them some more, a comfortable quiet spreading between them once again

All too soon, the sound of feet coming up the steps interrupted the silence.

"Nate's office is right up here," Frankie's voice came to them from the hall, growing louder.

"Do you have customers?" Jen looked to Nate.

"Oh, I totally forgot." He put his pictures away and attempted to straighten up his office even more than it already was. "I'll see you on Saturday, right?"

"Yeah. I'll see you then." Jen headed towards the door.

"Thanks again."

"Anytime. Bye." She stopped in the doorway to wave.

Nate stopped what he was doing and looked her in the eyes.

"Bye."

CHAPTER FIFTEEN

A ll right, Molly, why don't we take a few of you and your daughter together? Morgan, could you go stand by your Mom?"

It was mid-July, and without a doubt, the hottest day of the year. The wedding ceremony of Molly and Fred Burke had just ended, and the newly married couple and Molly's daughter, Morgan, were having family photographs taken at the downtown zoo. The newlyweds had opted to not have a bridal party at all, but to keep it more of a family affair. As Jen stood baking in the sun, she couldn't have been happier that she only had three people to worry about photographing.

"That's great. Now give your Mom a hug," she instructed the six year old girl.

The red-headed bride embraced her daughter.

"Lovely," Jen approved. "Why don't we all move towards the fountains, and do some poses there."

Together the four of them walked. Jen dabbed the sweat from her forehead with a tissue, in an attempt to rescue what little makeup she still wore. The welcome sound of splashing water signaled that they were close to their destination.

"Mom, can I go play in the fountains?" Morgan begged.

"Honey, these are for looking at, not playing in," Molly explained.

"But it's so hot," she whined.

"Come here, Morgan." Fred waved her towards him.

When she got near enough, he picked her up and placed her on the low stone wall that surrounded one of the fountain pools.

"Hold my hand," he instructed. "Now lean in towards the water, and you can touch it to cool off a little."

Morgan complied, and began swinging her free hand through the squirting water.

Fred looked to his wife. "It's hot out here, especially in dress clothes, and she's been so good."

Molly nodded and placed her hand on her husband's back.

"Thanks Daddy." Morgan splashed the water around.

Jen, trying not to get choked up, masked her emotions by covering her face with her camera and taking a picture with Fred and Morgan playing together in the foreground, and Molly in the background, glowing as she watched her family interact.

When the lump in Jen's throat had subsided, she continued directing the photo shoot. "Okay, should we finish up?"

"Sure," Fred answered. "It's time to hop down, Morgan." He lifted her off the step and set her on the ground.

"We'll be fast, I promise," Jen reassured the little girl. "Molly and Fred, why don't you two have a seat on the edge of the fountain, and Morgan, you sit down between your parents on the ground."

The trio's eyes sparkled with gladness, and the freckles of the fair-skinned girls dotted the apples of their upturned cheeks.

"That's nice. Fred, could you put your arm around Molly's waist, and your other hand on Morgan's shoulder?"

Jen pressed the button and snapped another picture.

After a few more photos of Molly and Fred together near the water, the bride and groom decided it was too hot to continue and stopped for the day. As they left the zoo, Jen couldn't help but stop and capture one last image of the family as they walked away, arms around each other, bouquets clutched in the outer hand of each girl, dropping petals as they strolled toward the park's exit.

Once in her car, Jen vowed to herself to get her air

conditioning fixed as soon as possible. The heat was unbearable, and the air inside was heavy and humid. She retrieved a beverage from her grocery bag and drank down every drop of the now warm and syrupy liquid. Finally, having rolled down the window on every door, she put the car into drive and made her way to the Manor, savoring even the slightest breeze that blew through her car.

Before entering the hall, Jen stopped in the restroom in an effort to try to make herself look more presentable. After combing her windblown hair and freshening her makeup, she left the bathroom and pushed open the French doors to the grand ballroom. The dry, cool air felt good. Without hesitation, she made a beeline for the bar where she saw Nate also approaching.

"Hi, guys." She greeted Nate, and Matty, who was getting glasses lined up for the undoubtedly busy cocktail hour about to begin.

"Hey, Jen," Nate replied.

"Hi, Babe. You look so hot," Matty flirted.

"It's nearly a hundred degrees out, Matty. Everyone looks hot." She was not in the mood for his antics.

Nate gave a short, but snickering laugh. Matty shot him a dirty look that Nate returned with a large grin and apologetic raise of his hand.

"Can I just have a cranberry juice, please?"

"You know what I mean, though," Matty continued, trying to recover, using the same voice she had heard him use a thousand times while charming one woman or another, "like the way this kind of clings to you." He reached across the bar to pull the fabric of her lightweight, cream-colored blouse away from her damp skin.

Jen saw where Matty's wandering hand headed and jumped back.

"I don't think so," Jen snapped.

Just as she moved out of the way, Matty's hand narrowly missing his desired target, Jen saw, from the corner of her eye, Nate lunge forward from the opposite end of the bar. In an instant, he was behind it, grabbing Matty's outstretched arm.

"Let's keep our hands to ourselves, shall we?" Nate's voice was stern and startling, a tone Jen had never expected to hear out of him.

She watched in stunned silence as Matty yanked his forearm from Nate's grasp and looked at him, as if contemplating whether or not a fight would be a wise idea. After a moment, Matty broke the stare and turned away from Nate, who had not yet looked away.

The tension eased, and Nate put his attention back on Jen.

"Now, what was it you wanted to drink?" Nate's voice returned to normal, though he eyed Matty suspiciously.

Still in shock by what had just happened, Jen could barely form words.

"Umm...Cran...Cranberry juice, please."

Nate reached down to select a glass, but Matty interrupted him.

"Hey. Only bartenders are supposed to be back here." Matty pushed Nate aside.

"Had you been doing your job, I wouldn't be back here," Nate retorted.

Looking under the bar again, Nate came back with two glasses in hand. One empty and one full.

"What's this?" he demanded.

"How should I know?" Matty snapped.

"Well, it looks to me like a glass of whiskey, and seeing as only bartenders are allowed behind the bar, and you're the only one here, I'm guessing it's yours."

"Prove it," Matty shot back.

It was Jen's turn to laugh. "I'm pretty sure he just did."

"What are you going to do about it?" Matty pressed.

"I'm not going to do anything." Nate was calm. "Unless you don't turn around and leave right now. In that case I'll be informing our employer that you've been both drinking on the job, and stealing, as I assume you haven't been paying for all this liquor."

Matty hesitated for a second before accepting

defeat. In a final act of defiance, he grabbed the glass from Nate's hand, splashing most of the whiskey out of it, and then, after throwing back the rest of the liquor, he hurled the empty glass, smashing it against the wall before finally turning on his heel to walk out.

Neither Jen nor Nate spoke a word until Matty was out of the room. Once he had slammed the door behind him, Nate knelt down to pick up the shards of glass. Jen rushed around the counter and knelt down in front of him.

"Nate," she said softly, as she touched his hand, stopping him from picking up pieces and causing him to look her in the eyes, "thank you. That was..."

"Pathetic?" he finished for her.

"No. I mean yes, Matty was pathetic, but you were...incredible. Thank you for watching out for me."

Nate seemed embarrassed and looked away. He returned to picking up glass, this time with Jen's help.

"I was sure for a second there that you two were going to fight," she said, in a lighter tone.

"Nah." Nate sounded more at ease, pretending his encounter with Matty hadn't come as close to blows as it had.

"Well, it's lucky for Matty you didn't," Jen added, still a little in awe of Nate's rougher side.

Nate chuckled.

"Thanks for the vote of confidence, but it's been

quite a while since I've fought anyone."

"That's probably because you are so good at handling situations like that. I can't believe you were able to talk him into just walking out of here. You were really calm."

"Speaking of him walking out of here," Nate said, "we'll have to let my uncle and Frankie know that they need to call another bartender in here for tonight."

"Oh, you're right. I can finish cleaning this up, if you want to go talk to them," Jen offered.

"Do you mind? I probably should."

"Not at all."

"Thanks." Nate stood up.

"Nate." Jen stood with him. "Thank you again, for looking out for me."

"Always." Nate gave her a wink and a poke with his elbow before walking away towards the kitchen to relay the day's events to Frankie and Al.

CHAPTER SIXTEEN

The following Monday, Jen was still thinking about the encounter between Nate and Matty. In the past when Jen had seen men fight, it was always a turn off, something she considered a sign of immaturity. Somehow, this was different. Nate had jumped to her aid. No one had ever done that before; at least, no man had. Though she still didn't care for the idea of people hurting each other, if she was honest with herself, she had to admit that deep down, a part of her liked that someone cared that much about her.

The sound of her ringing phone jolted Jen out of her thoughts and back to the image on her monitor, which she'd been blankly staring at rather than editing. Happy for the distraction from her work, she jumped out of her chair and ran to the other side of the room where her purse lay. By the time she retrieved it from the bottom of her bag, it had already rung four times. Without checking the caller ID, Jen flipped it open to stop it from going to voice mail.

"Hello?" She moved to the center of the room

where she knew the signal was best.

"Hey, Jen. It's Nate."

A brief, but distinct, rush of excitement ran through her veins at the sound of his voice.

"Hi. I was just thinking about you."

"Oh, no. Good stuff I hope."

"Not really," Jen teased with her best imitation of disgust.

Nate laughed.

"So what's going on?" Jen prompted after a second.

"I was just wondering if you'd want to hang out one day this week to watch a movie or something?"

"Sure, that'd be great. What'd you have in mind?"

"Well, have you seen Camp Coocoopa yet?"

"Nope."

"I could bring that," he suggested.

"That sounds fun."

"Perfect. When's good for you?"

"Well, Claire and I are doing a girl night thing tonight, but are you free tomorrow?"

"Definitely. I'll bring dinner. Is six good?"

"Absolutely. If you're bringing the movie and dinner, then at least let me take care of dessert."

"All right," he agreed. "Cool. I'll see you tomorrow. Oh, is there anything you don't like to eat?"

"Well, I can't eat any kind of fish, since I'm

allergic, but other than that it's all good."

"Okay, great. I'll see you then."

"Yeah, see ya, then. Bye."

"Bye."

Jen hung up the phone and dropped down onto one of the worn couch cushions, letting out a long sigh as she sank in. *Is this a date?*

Replaying the conversation in her head, she thought back on exactly what Nate's words were and how he sounded. *He wasn't at all nervous. Then again, neither was I. He asked if I wanted to hang out, not go out. Friends hang out, dates go out. If this was a date, he would've made it clear,* she told herself, but she still ran through their conversation in her mind a few more times to be certain. Afterwards, Jen again concluded that their movie night would in fact be two friends hanging out, and it would be best that way. As friends, she was never nervous around Nate. As friends, she had someone to make casual conversation with at work, and someone to hang out with during the week. As friends, she had someone who she could call on when she needed help, and someone who could call her when he needed it. *Our friendship is great, and I don't want more than that. Do I?*

* * * * *

Standing in front of her closet the next day, Jen contemplated what to wear, wishing Claire was there to help her decide.

Her roommate had left a note that morning, making a feeble attempt at an excuse as to why she wouldn't be home until very late that evening. Knowing her friend all too well, Jen read between the lines and was certain Claire saw this as a date and wanted to make herself scarce. The idea made Jen anxious, and she tried, instead, to focus on the clothing in front of her.

Finally, she decided on her favorite pale blue, belted, ruffled shirt dress. It was cute, not to mention comfortable, and Jen always felt her best when wearing it. Taking a few more minutes in the bathroom than usual, she straightened her hair and touched up her makeup.

The buzzer rang and sent Jen running to the front door.

"Hello?" she spoke into the intercom.

"Hi. It's me," Nate's voice answered.

"Come on up."

Jen used the several minutes it took Nate to reach the sixth floor to retrieve the cupcakes from the fridge, along with some plates and glasses from the cupboard.

She spent the morning baking her very favorite dessert, a spicy carrot cupcake. Each cake had been perfectly piped with a swirl of the lightest, fluffiest cream cheese frosting Jen had ever made, and then dusted with sparkling sugar crystals.

When his knock came, she walked barefoot across the wood floor to the door and opened it.

"Hi." She smiled.

"Hi."

"Wow! What did you bring?" Jen was surprised when she saw Nate holding three brown paper bags in his hands and a plastic one hanging over his arm. "Here, let me take some of that." She reached for a bag.

"Thanks. It's Chinese," he answered. "That's okay, right?"

"Are you kidding? That's great," she replied with fervor. "Come on in. Let's eat. I'm starved."

"Me, too." Nate followed Jen into the kitchen.

Together they placed the paper bags on the counter. As Nate opened them up, Jen peeked inside each one, only to see indistinguishable white to-go containers.

"What would you like to drink?" She offered him a variety of beverages.

"Iced tea would be good," he answered.

Jen filled two glasses with ice and then some iced green tea from the refrigerator, while Nate removed container after container from the bags.

After a moment, he began to laugh.

"What is it?" She handed him his drink.

"I'm just thinking I may have over-bought. When they put like forty fortune cookies and sets of chopsticks in the bag, you know they think you're buying for a lot of people."

"Ha ha. Yeah, I'd say so."

"Well, in my defense, I didn't know if Claire would be here, so I bought for the three of us."

"Aww. That was thoughtful. Actually, she's having dinner with some work friends tonight."

"More for us, I guess." He shrugged. "Let's dish some of this out. I wasn't sure if their egg rolls had shrimp in them, so I got spring rolls instead. I hope that's all right."

"I love spring rolls, and thanks for remembering." Jen took one from the folded paper box he offered her.

"You do realize you did just tell me what you were allergic to, like, a day ago, right?" He laughed.

"You'd be surprised how quickly some people forget, or maybe don't care to remember in the first place." Jen thought of her first date with Steve.

They filled their plates with mounds of vegetable fried rice, pepper steak, boneless spare ribs, steamed dumplings, and sesame chicken, until no room remained for anything else. Jen pulled a stool from one side of the counter to the other, and sat down opposite Nate, the spread of to-go containers, fortune cookies, napkins, and chopsticks between them.

"Oh wow. This is so good," Jen exclaimed, after her first bite of juicy pepper steak.

"Glad you like it. It's from my favorite Chinese place, Ling's. It's right down the street from here."

A momentary silence fell between them, and for the briefest instant Jen couldn't help but imagine how nice it would be if Nate's favorite Chinese place became *their* favorite Chinese place.

"Whatcha thinkin'?" Nate looked at her curiously as he dipped the dumpling he was holding with his chopsticks into the dish of soy sauce that sat between them.

"Oh, nothing. Just enjoying the food," she lied, not wanting to admit the truth.

"Okay." Nate looked at her with a sly and suspicious grin.

The look made Jen wonder if he knew she wasn't being honest, and was deciding whether or not to give her a hard time about it. Not wanting to give him the chance, she changed the subject.

"Hey, quit hogging all the sauce." She playfully pushed his dumpling out of her way with her own.

"I was here first. You're gonna have to fight me for it," he kidded back.

Jen faked right with her chopsticks, and then left, causing Nate to try and block her way, before scooting her dumpling underneath his and dunking it into the sauce, then finally popping it into her mouth.

"Mmm," she nodded as she chewed. "The sweet taste of victory."

"Ah, I let you win." Nate waved his own now empty chopstick at her.

"Keep telling yourself that," Jen replied with a playful smirk, before washing down her last bite with a sip of iced tea.

Again, a comfortable quiet filled the air and Nate looked around the room to take in his surroundings for the first time since he arrived. A puzzled look crossed his face, and Jen followed his gaze to the large corkboard covered in photos of cupcakes.

"Those are nice pictures. Did you take them? What am I saying?" He looked a little embarrassed. "Of course you took them. You're a great photographer."

"Thanks."

"Where'd you get all the cupcakes?"

"Claire and I make them." Jen shrugged modestly.

"What? No you don't." Nate stood up to take a closer look at the collection.

"Ha ha. Yes we do. See?"

Jen walked to the opposite counter and picked up the tray of cupcakes she had made earlier that day, bringing them over to where she and Nate had been sitting.

"Those are amazing."

"Thanks. Cupcakes are kind of our thing," she said nonchalantly. "We take a class together on Thursday nights to learn different baking techniques.

On Mondays we just kind of make up our own recipes and try them out. The ones that make the wall are our favorites." She motioned to the board.

"Cool."

Nate looked them over more closely, with Jen at his side.

"Which one do you like best?"

"Well, aesthetically speaking, I was pretty happy with this one." She pointed to a recent photograph. "It was dark chocolate with espresso mousse filling. I'm not gonna lie, it tasted pretty amazing, too." She giggled. "But if you're talking purely taste, the ones I made today, carrot cake, those are my favorites."

"So what are we waiting for?" Nate questioned. "Let's dig into one of those."

"Here." She handed him one.

"It almost looks too good to eat." He gave her a sideways grin. "Almost."

Jen watched as he carefully pulled the paper away from the bottom of the cake, removing it completely from the wrapper before tasting it. He opened his mouth wide and sunk his teeth into the moist cake, taking a colossal bite.

"Mmm." He sat down on the stool, closing his eyes as he chewed. "Mmm," he exclaimed again. "Seriously, this is incredible." After a few moments, the cupcake was gone.

"Wow, if you weren't such a great photographer,

I'd say you should go into business making these."

"Aww. Thanks."

"Honestly, I've never had such a good carrot cake," he raved.

"Now you're just being nice."

"No way," he assured her. "Do you mind if I have another?"

"Help yourself." She passed him the plate and took their empty dinner plates to the sink. "Do you want to go have them in the living room and we can watch our movie?"

"Sure. Let me help you clean up first, though." He set the cupcake back down.

"Thanks."

Together they closed up the leftover boxes of Chinese and stacked them neatly on the counter, ready to be broken into during the movie should they decide they wanted to pick at some leftovers.

"Do you want some coffee or milk with dessert?"

"Coffee would be great."

"I'll make some. How do you take it?"

"Cream, no sugar, please. I'll get the movie set up while you do that."

"Okay."

Jen brought two large mugs of coffee and set them on the table in front of the couch. "Oh, forgot the cupcakes." She went back to the kitchen. "Just take either coffee. They're both the same," she said over her shoulder.

Jen grabbed the tray of cupcakes in one hand and stack of napkins in the other.

Nate sat near the center of the couch. After picking up a cupcake, Jen sat down next to him and curled her legs under her. They were sitting close. As Jen settled in, she realized her thigh was up against Nate's. Suddenly she was very aware of how near she was to him and wondered if he noticed it, too. She leaned her back against the rear couch cushion and her shoulder brushed against his.

"You ready?" Nate's voice broke the silence.

"Oh yeah," Jen answered.

Nate pressed play and the previews began. By the time the opening credits ended Nate appeared already amused. The comedy, that in Jen's opinion was funny enough to begin with, grew more so to her, as she caught Nate's contagious laughter. An hour and a half later, after stopping briefly to bring the leftovers to the couch, the pair leaned back, to-go containers on their laps, lungs aching from roaring with laughter, and completely content.

"You were right," Jen started, "that movie was a riot."

"I'm glad you liked it. So what's your favorite comedy?"

"I...can't say. It's too embarrassing."

"What? Oh come on. How bad could it be?"

"Pretty bad."

"Just tell me. If you don't I'll just look through your DVD's till I find it." He leaned forward to get up.

"Okay. Okay." Jen grabbed his arm, and pulled him back down to the couch before he could get too far. "Life on the Farm."

She covered her face, pretending to be humiliated.

"The one with that guy, Johnny Skyline in it?"

"Yes." Jen looked up again.

"Oh. That *is* bad. No wonder you're embarrassed."

"Hey." She grabbed a pillow from the end of the couch and hit him in the chest with it.

"I'm just kidding. I've never even see it. We should watch that one next time."

"Yeah."

The room grew quiet, and Jen swept her light strands of hair to one side of her face and twisted them.

"Well, I should probably get going." Nate slapped his hands on his thighs, before getting up.

"All right." Jen followed suit and stood, too. "Thanks for hanging out and for bringing dinner. This was great."

"Yeah, it was," Nate agreed.

After packing up the leftovers together and placing them in the fridge, Nate made his way to the door, DVD in hand.

"So we've got Emma and Aaron's beach wedding this weekend, don't we?" Nate stuck his free hand into his pocket.

"Yep."

"That should be a good one."

He paused, and for a moment, neither of them spoke.

"Well, thanks for everything." He took a step toward her. "I'll see ya this weekend." He leaned in and gave her a quick hug.

"Yeah. See ya," Jen said quietly.

"Night." Nate opened the door, gave her a small wave, and then turned down the hall towards the stairs.

"Night."

CHAPTER SEVENTEEN

The wedding of Emma and Aaron was one that Jen looked forward to more than any other. Over the last few weeks she had often envisioned what the ceremony would look like taking place on the beach, the sun setting in the distance. Jen pictured the night as it would progress and how the couple would gaze into each other's eyes as they shared their first dance. She imagined the collection of guests that would mingle together on the sand, enjoying delectable hors d'oeuvres, and light music that would float through the air. Most of all, she contemplated the photographs she wanted to take in order to capture it all. It would be the perfect wedding. While other events certainly had their inspirational moments, it was rare that Jen felt inspired as an artist by an entire affair, and even less often had she been hired for such an occasion by a couple who genuinely seemed to be an exquisite match for each other, not to mention pleasant to work for.

When the date arrived, it did not disappoint.

From the moment Jen stepped out onto the beach, she was in awe of the gorgeous ceremony setting. A circle of white paper lanterns sat in the sand and encompassed the area with a warm glow. In the center, two dozen fine gold chairs, half on one side and half on the other, created a walkway for the bride. The aisle was lined with several posts in the sand to which sheer white fabric was tied, suspended effortlessly in the breeze. It was elegant and simple.

"Is this incredible or what?" Nate's smooth voice came from behind her.

"It's extraordinary," she exclaimed, pulling her eyes away from the setting to look up at Nate.

"Did you see the rest?"

"No." Jen realized she hadn't yet left the spot where she stood.

"Come on." Nate motioned with this arm and walked out of the lanterns' circle and down the beach. "Here's where the reception will be." He gestured when they approached a larger circle of paper lanterns.

Although, there was still a fair amount of daylight, the glow from the lanterns reflected and flickered in the golden accents that dressed the area. Inside the ring of lanterns was a semicircle of tables, each set for four guests. The Ivy Manor's finest white china, with gold leaf inlay, brought elegance to the setting. In the center of each table sat a simple spherical vase filled with water, sea glass, and a floating candle. Across from the dining area stood a string of buffet tables, bar, and Nate's DJ stand, all well lit by a line of lustrous tiki torches.

"Pretty great, huh?" Nate stuffed his hands in his pockets and let out a contented sigh as he enjoyed the view.

"Sure is. Has Aaron seen it yet? I know Emma can't wait."

"Yeah, he was by earlier this afternoon with his dad getting things settled with the rental company." Nate looked to Jen. "So how did Emma's getting-ready pictures go today?"

"Very well. Thanks for asking. Everything happened right on schedule, and she was super excited. That always makes the picture taking a lot easier."

"I'm glad. It sounds like it was a good day for you."

"It was. Well, they'll be here soon, so I should get set. See you after the ceremony."

"Yep. Good luck."

* * * * *

As guests arrived, the mood was warm and relaxed, just as Jen remembered Emma saying she hoped it would be.

Aaron's cousins stood in the background strumming on their guitars as guests entered. Finally, when the sun was getting low in the sky, and the shadows along the sand and stones were long, Aaron entered with the Justice of the Peace and the rest of the bridal party. A momentary silence fell as the guitarists paused before beginning their next piece. Quietly, they picked out notes, the sound growing and mingling with the crash of the lake's waves on the shore. Just as the swell of music reached its peak, Emma came into view. Guests murmured as they took in the bride. Emma looked lovely. Her white dress was unlike any other Jen had seen. The lightweight lace fell just below her knee in the front and seemed to sweep down ever so slightly in the back, creating the illusion of a train. Her short veil lifted gently off her hair with each breeze. Best of all, happiness radiated from her face.

The rest of the ceremony was equally enchanting, and when Emma and Aaron strolled arm in arm back down the aisle, an array of pinks, purples, and blues painting the sky in the backdrop, Jen artistically captured the moment.

"That was the most fantastic ceremony I have ever photographed," Jen said to the couple when they approached her. "Congratulations."

"Thank you," they replied in unison, still holding each other.

"Are you ready for more pictures?"

"Yeah, our family's over there waiting." Emma

pointed.

"Great. Let's head down the beach and get some photos while we still have this gorgeous sunset," Jen suggested.

Jen worked with the family members to get all of the formal shots needed and then followed up with several playful ones of Emma and Aaron.

"Okay, you two," she instructed, "stand over here, and Aaron pick Emma up in your arms."

Aaron swept his bride off her feet, and Jen pressed down the shutter button, as Emma and her delicate dress were lifted in the air. After a quick kiss on her cheek, he placed her gently on the sand.

"Stay right here. I have an idea." Jen turned towards the ground to find a stick. "This will do." She picked one up.

"What's that for?" Emma and Aaron laughed.

"Just wait."

In the sand Jen wrote the words "Just Married" and drew a large heart around them, then laid the stick down nearby as if it were an artist's brush.

"All right, now come and stand in the heart."

"Oh, this is so cute." Emma gushed, as she and her new husband obeyed.

"Perfect." Jen photographed their feet in the sand just as a hint of a wave came up on the shore. "Well, we're about out of light, so would you like to head to your reception?"

"Sounds good." Aaron nodded.

As she neared the reception area, Jen could see the celebration was in full swing. Guests dotted the center of the lantern-lit circle, chatting and dancing, drinks in hand. Jen could make out Nate and Frankie at the far side of the ring, laughing heartily as they joked with each other.

"Things sure seem to be going well over here," Jen observed aloud when she approached the two men. ·

"They sure are," Frankie agreed. "They love the food." He patted himself on the back.

"They always do," Jen complimented.

"Speaking of which..." Nate turned and retrieved a plate from a nearby table. "Angie made up a plate of hors d'oeuvres for us."

Jen selected a stuffed mushroom from the plate. "So what's the plan for the evening?" She spoke between bites.

"Here's the schedule." Nate handed her the list of events for the evening. "I'll announce their first dance whenever you're set."

"Ready when you are." Jen gave him a thumbs-up after looking over the rest of the items on the sheet.

"Ladies and Gentleman," Nate began, "please draw your attention to our newlyweds Emma and Aaron as they share their first dance together as husband and wife."

The couple's friends and family applauded and

cheered as Aaron led Emma to the center of the circle, twirling her under his arm before drawing her close. Jen captured photos of the couple as they embraced and swayed barefoot in the sand. After a minute or so, Nate invited the best man and maid of honor to join the newly married couple. Together, the pairs talked and laughed as they danced and soaked in the moment.

When the song ended, Nate changed the music and an upbeat number took its place. Then in his best radio host voice, he called for all the single ladies to join Emma front and center. Jen smiled as she watched Nate become more comfortable in his less serious role.

"All right, ladies, are you ready?" he called.

Emma's small but enthusiastic group of single friends cheered.

"And Emma, are you ready?"

The bride held her bouquet in the air and shook it, nodding her head.

"On three. One.Two.Three..."

She threw the bundle of flowers high into the air and, just as it left her fingertips, Jen pressed the shutter, then turned towards the group of girls with their outstretched arms to capture their reaction. From the center of the crowd, a hand emerged, raising the flowers triumphantly into the sky, as the rest clapped around her.

"That went well," Nate remarked to Jen as she came around the DJ stand, when the celebrating had begun to die down.

"I agree," Jen beamed. "I like that voice you do."

"What voice?"

"You know, the one you just did. Your radio host voice. Ladies, are you ready?" Jen imitated Nate's earlier speech.

"Oh, no." He laughed. "Is that what I sound like?"

"No. Yours is way better. It's fun. I like it," she repeated.

"Well, thanks," Nate answered sheepishly with a bit of an embarrassed smile. "Do you think they've settled down enough to do the cake cutting?" he asked, changing the subject.

"Yeah. I'm gonna go over there." Jen pointed to the cake as she walked that way.

Just as she reached the table, Nate's usual smooth voice returned and informed everyone that the cake cutting was about to begin.

Jen positioned herself and got ready for her favorite moment. After capturing a picture of the couple's hands together, sliding the knife through the cake, Jen caught a glimpse of Nate. Although he was stuck behind the DJ stand, she noticed him standing as tall as he could, craning his neck to watch the couple. Carefully, they both lifted a bite-sized piece of the dessert towards each other and then simultaneously fed one another, intentionally missing a bit in their aim. The crowd applauded, and, as always, soon after returned to their seats.

As Emma giggled and licked the frosting off her fingers, Aaron moved in, and, careful not to touch her dress with his icing-covered digits, wrapped an arm around her, lifted her off her feet, and kissed her sweetly on the lips. When Jen turned around, Nate's eyes were on her. He lifted his hands to his face miming a camera as he mouthed the words "good one." Jen nodded and grinned back.

When dinner finished, Jen took photographs of the guests dancing together and enjoying the evening, as Nate played request after request.

"What a great wedding," Jen sighed after a long series of party pictures.

"Sure is," Nate agreed.

She took the camera from around her neck and put it down on the table nearby. Then, grabbing a chair, she brought it next to where Nate stood and sat down, rolling her head from side to side to relieve her sore muscles.

"What an amazing night." Nate looked up towards the dark sky. "I can't believe how many stars you can see."

Jen sighed again and leaned back, tilting her head to gaze at the stars as she drank in the warm summer night.

"It's perfect," she whispered.

The sound of someone approaching the stand interrupted their thoughts and jolted Jen back to reality.

"You two have been so great." Jen heard Emma's voice.

"Thanks," Nate replied.

"But you've been working too hard. You need to take a break."

"Ha ha. No worries there." Jen laced her fingers behind her head and leaned back to indicate her clearly relaxed state.

"No, I mean you need to have fun. Come dance."

"Oh, we're all right. But thanks," Jen answered politely.

"I won't take no for an answer." Emma gave her best attempt at a firm look.

"Looks like she means business." Nate chuckled as he adjusted the playlist. "Come on."

"Good." Emma turned away, clearly pleased with herself.

Nate reached his hand out to Jen.

"May I?"

Jen answered by giving him her hand. It felt small inside of his, as he entwined her slender fingers with his own. Hand in hand, he led her out to the center of the lantern-lit area as Twilight Nocturne played.

"Did you?" Jen motioned towards the speakers.

"Maybe." Nate looked pleased.

"Thanks...I love this song."

"I know," he said softly.

Nate stopped and gently pulled her toward him. Jen's heart began to race. Nate wrapped his free arm around her waist and rested his hand on the small of her back. Jen lifted her free hand to his shoulder and placed it on his arm. Slowly they swayed back and forth in the sand. Jen did all she could to control her breathing as she became more and more aware of Nate's strong arm around her. After a moment, he rested their entwined hands on his chest and pulled her closer. Nearer to him now than ever before, she rested her head on his chest. She was completely aware of all her senses — the way his dress shirt felt under her fingertips, the way his rolled up sleeves showed the muscles in his arm next to her own thin frame. The intoxicating scent of his faint cologne mingled with the clean freshness of his shirt. Closing her eyes, she listened for the sound of his heartbeat, hoping its steadiness would slow hers, only to find his pounding as hard and as fast as her own. Everyone and everything around them seemed to disappear. There were no guests, no music, no waves beating on the shore, just Nate.

As quickly as it had come, the moment was gone. The song had ended and a new upbeat one had taken its place. Jen stood motionless, still holding onto Nate, as if hoping to get the moment back. She felt as if she had suddenly awoken from a dream. Slowly, he released her, letting his arm fall to the side and separating his hand from hers. Jen looked up at him, and he down at her, neither speaking nor stepping away.

Nate's voice was quiet and constricted. "Thank you...for the dance."

"Thank you." Jen looked up into his eyes.

"Are you the DJ?" A loud voice called from a few yards away.

Broken out of their intimate moment, Nate and Jen both turned their heads towards the voice.

"Yes."

"Could you play that one cha-cha song?" The intoxicated guest requested more loudly than necessary.

"Sure." Nate forced a cheerful expression and nodded at the man, then returned his gaze to Jen.

"I'm sorry..." he began softly, disappointment written clearly on his face.

"No. No. It's fine," Jen assured him. "You...we need to work."

At first, Nate didn't say anything, but instead continued to look deeply into her eyes. Jen felt her heart begin to pound once again.

"Are you free tomorrow?" There was a sound of longing in his voice.

Jen wracked her brain, trying to recall what day tomorrow even was.

"I'm sorry." She let out a deep breath. "My parents, they just got back from months of being away, and Claire and I are supposed to go over to see them, and..." she rambled.

"No, it's okay. Family's important," he reassured her.

"Would you want to come?" she blurted.

"Yes." Nate's face lit up. "I'd love to."

"Great." Jen breathed a sigh of relief and looked, eyes sparkling, up at him.

"Well, I better..." Nate trailed off, as he pointed a thumb towards the DJ stand.

"Oh, yeah. Go."

Taking one last look at her, Nate turned and walked toward his station. After a few steps he stopped. He turned and mouthed, "Thanks."

CHAPTER EIGHTEEN

The next morning, while Jen drove herself home from church, her mind raced as she tried to organize what seemed to be millions of thoughts running through her head at once, all of which centered around one topic: Nate.

What is going on? It's like all this time we were friends. We acted like friends. We talked like friends, and then we have one dance together and BAM! There are all these feelings. Could it just have been the moment? It was an incredibly romantic setting. Would any two people have felt something, or was it because it was him? Her heartbeat quickened and her head felt dizzy with anticipation. *I need to talk to him the first chance I get,* she resolved.

Knowing she was just moments away from seeing Nate, Jen's stomach did flip-flops as she neared her apartment. *Okay, I've got five minutes to get freshened up before he gets here.* She glanced at the clock. *Then maybe we can get a few moments alone before we go to my parents'.*

After parking her car, she ran upstairs, taking the

last flight two at a time. Swinging the door open, Jen stopped dead in her tracks, sweating and out of breath.

"Hey, Lady," Claire greeted from her favorite arm chair.

"Morning." Nate beamed at her from the couch.

The sight of Nate made Jen even more confused. *What am I going to say to him?*

"Are you all right?" Nate asked when she didn't speak.

"Oh, I'm sorry. Hi...to both of you. Yeah, I'm fine. Just lost in thought, and I ran up the stairs, and..." Jen trailed off. "Anyway, would you two mind giving me a couple of minutes, before we go?"

"Go ahead." Claire shrugged.

"Thanks," Jen called, already heading down the hall.

Once in her bedroom, she closed the door behind her and leaned against it, letting out a long sigh.

Okay, she said to herself. *You can talk to him later. Now just isn't the right time.* She rested her head on the wooden frame behind her.

Jen closed her eyes and relaxed as she pictured his face, the friendly grin she had grown so accustomed to, and the sound of his voice. After a moment she felt much more like herself.

Taking a quick look in her mirror, Jen dabbed her forehead with a tissue, touched up her blush and went back out to meet her friends.

"Thanks for waiting."

"Sure thing," Claire replied. "You ready?"

"Yep."

"I can drive us," Nate offered, as he stood up.

"Oh, you don't have to," Jen dissuaded.

"I don't mind at all. Let's go."

Together the three of them left the apartment and headed towards the stairs.

"No remark about us taking the stairs?" Claire inquired of Nate.

"Nah. I figure I've got legs, I might as well use them," he replied, quoting Jen and giving her a wink.

"Sounds like someone else I know." Claire gave Jen a sly look.

"I'm parked right over there." Nate motioned to his SUV when they came out the building's door.

Claire walked to the back passenger side, and Nate unlocked and opened it for her, waiting for her to slide in and closing it behind her.

He leaned in close to Jen as he reached for the handle to open her door as well.

"Hi," he whispered in her ear.

"Hi." She looked up and met his eyes.

They seemed so close to each other, and yet so far apart. Imagining that everything she was feeling was visible to everyone around her, Jen lingered for only a moment, then broke away to enter the SUV.

"So..." Nate initiated. "Claire was telling me that your parents have been gone for almost four months now."

"Yeah, this has been their longest trip yet."

"Do you know all the places they've been?"

"Some of them, but not all," Jen said. The mood lightened. "They call once a week or so, but that's more just to let me know all is well, and where they currently are."

"I see. Do they take a lot of pictures?"

"Tons."

"Cool."

"Speaking of pictures," Claire said, "how was the wedding last night?"

"Amazing," Jen answered fervently, for more than one reason.

"Yeah, it was great," Nate added.

The rest of the ride went quickly as Jen dotted their conversation about the previous night's wedding with directions to her parents' home.

"Here we are on the right." She pointed, and Nate slowed to turn into the driveway.

The three friends made their way up the front steps and to the door. Nate held it open for Claire to enter. As Jen followed, he briefly placed his hand on the small of her back to usher her in. The feeling of his strong, warm hand touching her so gently felt like a rush of electricity running up and down her spine.

"Bob, they're here," Jen's equally blonde mom called as she ran through the kitchen to her daughter. "Hi, Sweetie." She grabbed Jen in a big hug. "Oh, we missed you."

"I missed you too, Mom." Jen hugged her tightly back.

Jen's Dad, a trim man with more gray than brown in his hair, entered the room and joined the group, giving his daughter a bear hug.

Her mother continued greeting her guests. "Hi, Claire, honey. It's so good to see you again."

"You too, Debbie," Claire said earnestly.

"Mom, Dad, this is my friend Nate." Jen gestured towards where he stood.

"Hi, Mrs. Schuman, Mr. Schuman." Nate gave her mom a polite hug and offered her dad his hand. "I hope I'm not imposing, coming over after you haven't seen your daughter for so long."

"No, not at all," Debbie answered. "Jen told us last night that you were coming. We're so glad to have you."

"And just call us Bob and Debbie," Bob added.

"Thanks. I will."

"Well, come on and let's eat," Debbie prompted. "We've got quite the spread."

Bob led the way through the house and to the deck that ran along the back. In the center of the structure stood an oversized wooden table covered with a bright tablecloth, five place settings, a large bowl of prepared fruit, and two pitchers of juice.

"Have a seat, have a seat," Bob encouraged. "Pour yourselves something to drink and we'll get the rest of the food."

The three did as told and chatted as they poured themselves glasses full of cranberry and white grape juice. Claire pulled out a chair on one side of the table, Jen sat next to her, and Nate chose the seat across from Jen.

"Wow, Mom, you weren't kidding when you said you have quite the spread," Jen spoke, upon seeing her mother and father's arms full of serving dishes. "Here, let me help." She got up to carry some platters to the table.

"This looks delicious," Nate praised, as the five of them filled their plates with every brunch food imaginable.

"Wait till you taste it," Claire began. "They make the best food."

"You're sweet, Claire." Debbie patted her fondly on the hand.

"Okay, so tell us all about your trip from the beginning," Jen pressed, as she cut a bite of sausage for herself.

"We had the most fantastic time." Her mother put down her silverware and gestured with her hands.

"Our plan was to hit as many of the national

parks as we could, but honestly, we'd get so caught up in each one we visited that we would just end up staying there for days and days or sometimes weeks at a time," Bob told them.

"What a great adventure," Nate exclaimed.

"It was," Bob agreed before taking a long drink from his glass.

"So what parks did you make it to?" Claire asked.

"Let's see," Debbie said, "we spent the majority of our time at the Grand Canyon National Park, Crater Lake's park, and on the way to those two we stopped in Big South Fork."

"Big South Fork is in Kentucky, right?" Nate looked to Debbie.

"Yes. Have you been there?"

"Not to the park, no. I've been to a small town nearby it, and I always wanted to go there." He speared a piece of sausage with his fork and popped it in his mouth.

"Nate worked there on a volunteer labor team that traveled around the country," Jen said.

"That's great." Debbie looked impressed. "You should go down to the park some time. It's wonderful."

"I hope to," Nate replied.

Nate raised his eyes to Jen's and met hers across the table for a moment, then grinned bashfully.

"So, what did you do while you were at the

parks?" Claire resumed their conversation and helped herself to second waffle.

Bob chimed in. "Well, at the Grand Canyon we got a backcountry permit that allowed us to hike off the paths and camp where we wanted. That was the best part. We ended up spending weeks there." He put his bagel down on his plate and sighed. "There's nothing like getting away from absolutely everything, and just being surrounded by nature. You wouldn't believe the quiet."

His wife nodded in agreement. "The days we were traveling in the truck, we tried to stay off the beaten path and really see the rural areas of the country," Debbie contributed. "I think we saw every road side attraction, stopped at every garage sale, and ate at every tiny local diner we saw."

* * * * *

As the afternoon progressed Debbie and Bob regaled Jen and her friends with dish after delicious dish, as well as an abundance of stories, both humorous and exciting, of their several month journey.

"What do you say we get these plates out of the way?" Debbie suggested. "I think it's time for presents. You girls come help me." She looked over her shoulder as she walked towards the kitchen.

"So tell me, Claire," Debbie chatted as the three women brought in a stack of plates. "What's new in your life? How's work? Are you seeing anyone? How are your folks?"

Claire laughed at the line of questions. "Well, work is good. Not much new to report there. My Mom and Dad are doing well, though honestly we aren't close like you guys, so I don't hear from them much, and as far as seeing anyone, well there is this one guy."

"Oh. What's his name?"

"Emmitt."

"And where did you meet him?"

"At work."

"Are you talking about your boyfriend?" Jen teased when she came in with a second armload of dishes.

"It's not official yet," Claire blushed "but I think I'd like it to be."

"Really?" Jen placed the dishes next to the sink.

"Yeah." Claire nodded.

"Aw, Claire, I'm so happy for you." Jen gave her best friend a hug.

"Thanks. I'm so happy for you, too," she returned.

"What do you mean?" Jen pulled away and looked at Claire curiously.

"You and Nate. I mean, clearly you two are something, right?"

"I..." Jen didn't know what to say.

"Oh, honey." Her mother put her hands on her

daughter's arms. "We just love him already. How come you didn't mention to us you were seeing someone?"

"Because. Well..." Jen was still at a loss for words. "We're friends," she whispered, not wanting Nate to overhear. "I think I...but I don't know how he..."

"He doesn't know yet how you feel?" Claire finished for her.

"Yeah. In fact, I don't even know exactly how I feel. It's just kind of sudden."

"Well, it's obvious he's crazy about you," Claire assured her.

"You think?"

For the first time, Jen allowed the tiniest bit of hope to build up inside of her.

"Without a doubt," her Mom stated.

"Totally."

The sound of the screen door and the men's voices brought an abrupt end to their conversation.

"We're just here to bring out the gifts." Bob entered with Nate at his side. "We'll meet you back outside."

Not wanting to talk about the matter anymore, Jen used the opportunity to go back outdoors to gather the tablecloth and napkins, and to collect her thoughts. After a short while, Claire and her mom joined her, followed by her Dad and Nate, who were carrying something covered in a sheet, along with an additional bag of gifts.

"This is for your apartment." Debbie placed a hand on each of girl's backs and gently pressed them towards the mystery object.

Claire and Jen simultaneously lifted the sheet off it, revealing a small, beautiful, intricately carved table with spindly legs.

"Oh, it's gorgeous," Jen oohed.

"Just beautiful." Claire opened and closed the tiny drawer at the top. "Thank you so much."

"Yes, thank you. We love it. Where did you find it?"

"We took the scenic route home," Bob said, "and stopped at a bunch of estate sales along the way. This piece came out of a century home. They had a professional refinish it. We saw it and just couldn't pass it up."

"I'm glad you didn't. Thanks. It's great."

* * * * *

As late afternoon approached, Jen sat on the couch with her family and friends. All the pictures had been looked at, and dessert had been eaten. With a sigh she leaned her head back, completely relaxed.

"I think I need a nap," she joked, after stretching and letting out a huge yawn.

Her Dad nodded. "Sundays will do that to you."

"We should probably get going. We drove together and I don't want to keep these guys busy all day."

"Let me load your end table into the car." Her father stood and made his way towards the gift.

"I'll help," Nate offered, joining him. "Thank you both very much for having me, and for brunch. It was excellent. And it was great to finally meet you."

"Pleasure meeting you too, Nate." Debbie gave him a hug. "You're welcome here any time."

"Thanks." He hugged her back.

"Bye, Mom." Jen gave her an embrace.

"Bye, Honey. See you soon, Claire."

Claire hugged Debbie. "Thank you again for the table."

Together, the three of them climbed into Nate's SUV and traveled back to the girls' building. Full and sleepy, the ride was peaceful and quiet.

Sitting in the silence, Jen felt the anticipation of the conversation she knew she needed to have with Nate.

Before long, they reached their destination. Nate exited the car first and opened the back to remove the table. Jen ran ahead to open the building door for him.

"I think I'm going to ride it up." Nate motioned to the elevator. "I just don't want your new table to get bumped around trying to carry it up the stairs."

"Oh, of course. I'll go with you." Jen pressed the up arrow next to the sliding doors.

"See you up there." Claire headed to the steps.

Waiting in front of the elevator, side by side, neither of them spoke.

The dinging sound announced the arrival of their lift, and they both stepped inside, Jen making sure the door stayed open for Nate as he carried in her new table.

"So..." Jen began after a pause. "Do you have any plans for the rest of the day?"

"Actually, yeah." Nate's voice was quiet and a little tense. "I'm supposed to meet Al and Frankie about some business things."

"Oh."

Jen couldn't think of anything else to say. She was trying to hide how upset she felt. She wanted to speak to him, but in reality, feeling as confused as she was, had no idea what she would even say.

The elevator dinged again and the doors opened on Jen's floor. Nate picked the table up and carried it into her apartment.

"Thanks so much," she said when he was inside. "You can just leave it there. We'll need to find the best spot for it."

Nate placed the delicate table carefully on the floor.

"Can you..." Nate motioned towards the hall.

"Yeah." Jen's heart leapt and her breath caught up in her throat.

Together they walked out into the empty hallway and closed the door behind them. For a moment, neither of them said anything.

"I'm sorry I have to go. It's just, Al and Frankie are making me a partner, and..."

"Nate, that's great," Jen exclaimed. "I'm so happy for you." She stood on her toes and gave him a hug.

Jen closed her eyes as he hugged her tightly back.

"Thanks." He let her go, and looked sadly at her.

"Are you all right?"

"Yeah, I just have some other things on my mind." His voice was still tense.

"Do you want to talk?" Jen asked, feeling incredibly concerned.

"Yes, but not today. Soon, though. Can I call you this week?"

"Of course." Jen tried her best to give him an encouraging smile despite the feeling of worry building inside her.

Nate seemed to relax. "Thanks. I'll talk to you soon." He gave her another quick hug before turning towards the stairs.

"Bye." Jen waved.

* * * * *

That evening, as Jen laid in her bed, not even the calming sound of the lake's waves could lull her to sleep. Her mind filled with a thousand thoughts and questions.

How did I not know? Jen looked back on all of her conversations with Nate, every kind gesture, all his thoughtful words, and friendly smiles. He was incredible. The way he had spent his life meeting the needs of other people, working all over the country, and now helping his uncle, was inspiring to her. The love he had for his family and the value he found in those relationships were exactly the things Jen herself thought were most important. His thoughtfulness and constant consideration for her needs were things she never dreamed she would find in a man. His appreciation for her work, and the abilities she possessed as an artist, made her glad to be the person she was. No one else had ever made her feel like that.

As the hours drifted by, Jen pondered all his amazing qualities. She still wondered how she had remained so oblivious to the man he was all this time, and until recently, even been blind to his obvious good looks. But all in all, the overwhelming sense of confusion she had been feeling had left her. Jen was certain of one thing. She loved him.

CHAPTER NINETEEN

As dawn approached, Jen tossed and turned. Through the night she was overtaken by exhaustion, but only for a few minutes before being awoken again by her thoughts.

She pulled the covers tightly around her and lay on her side, watching the minutes tick by on her bedside clock. *All right, it's almost six,* she told herself. *Just a little longer and it'll be a decent hour. I'll get up, start my day, and stop thinking about him.* She knew the last part was a lie, but she tried to convince herself anyway.

The noise of her phone vibrating on the nightstand was an unexpected jolt to her senses.

"Hello?" She spoke sleepily into the phone, before checking the number.

"Hi."

The sound of Nate's voice was like a shot of adrenaline.

"It's Nate." He paused. "I'm sorry, I don't know what I was thinking calling this early. Go back to sleep. Sorry."

"Wait!" Jen practically shouted into the phone, afraid he would hang up. "Wait," she said again, this time much more quietly. "I couldn't sleep."

"Me neither." Nate was quiet for a moment. "Would you? I'm at Java Jane's right now. Would you want to get some coffee or something? We could take a walk."

"Definitely. I'll be there in a few minutes."

"Okay." Nate's voice sounded relieved, but not excited.

"K. Bye."

"Bye."

Jen unwrapped the sheet and comforter from around her and stepped barefoot onto the hardwood floor, the cool morning air chilling her skin. Taking a pair of jean shorts off the chair next to her bed and the hoodie that hung from the corner of her dresser mirror, she dressed and tiptoed across the hall to the bathroom, where she brushed her teeth and hair as quickly and quietly as she could.

A funny thought occurred to her as she stood looking into the bathroom mirror. All this time she had been convinced that a good relationship would be impossible to maintain without weekend dates and a typical work schedule, but in reality she and Nate had been dating each other all along. For months now, they had gotten dressed up and had an evening meal together on Saturday nights. They'd stayed in and watched movies, shared lunch, and met each other's families. Though it certainly wasn't how she imagined a relationship happening, she couldn't deny that it had. Now her only concern was whether Nate felt the same way.

After jotting a note to Claire, Jen left the apartment and headed down the stairs. The closer she got to the bottom, the slower she moved, the fear of uncertainty building up inside of her and making her feet heavier with every step she took closer to the exit.

Nate didn't sound like himself on the phone. His carefree demeanor had faded slightly in their last few conversations. *Could he suspect how I feel, and not feel the same way?* The thought was almost enough to make her run back up the stairs. *He's a good guy. Maybe he's trying to let me down easy. Especially now that he's going to be part owner of the Manor. He'll be my boss,* she realized. *He probably doesn't want to hurt my feelings, and he knows we'll have to keep working together.*

As she crossed the parking lot and neared Java Jane's, Jen saw Nate exit the coffee house and, head bowed, begin walking towards her, two cups of coffee in hand. Jen stuffed her own hands into the front pocket of her hoodie in an attempt to hide their trembling.

The sound of her footsteps alerted Nate to her presence, and his head shot up. Though she knew it was illogical, the moment his eyes met hers, Jen felt all of her fears melt away.

"Hi." He stopped in front of her, giving a nervous smile.

"Hi."

Jen didn't know what to do. She wanted to hug him, but felt awkward doing so when he hadn't moved.

"Oh, I brought you some coffee." He broke the silence.

"Thanks." She took it from him and tried to steady her hand before taking a sip. "Mmm. Cream, no sugar. You remembered," she said in a much lighter voice than she was actually feeling.

"Always," he whispered.

Both Nate and Jen paused, neither speaking, nor going anywhere. Nate shifted his weight from foot to foot, looking everywhere but at Jen.

"Do you want to walk?"

"Yes," Jen agreed without hesitation.

The pair began strolling away from the building and down the quiet side street toward the small lakefront park that stood near the coffee house. The sun peeked out from the horizon behind them, as they walked through the dewy grass to the water.

After a while, the silence was too much for her.

"So, how'd everything go at the Manor yesterday?" She felt unsure of what else to say. "Does it feel good to own a part of it?"

"Actually," Nate hesitated, "I'm not a partner yet."

"Oh." Jen didn't want to pry, but wondered what could have happened. "I'm sorry. I guess, I just thought it was kind of a done deal."

"Well, it still could be." Nate's tone had a hopeful uncertainty about it. "It's just there is something going on in my life. If things go the way I hope, well, that would be great." He sighed, chuckling quietly. "If they don't..." His face fell. "I just didn't want to commit to something, when there's the potential for an uncomfortable situation."

Nate swallowed hard.

Jen felt a sudden and indescribable fear at the thought of Nate leaving the Ivy Manor and not seeing him anymore.

"Want to sit down?" He pointed to a bench they had reached that stood facing the lake.

"Yeah."

Setting her coffee cup on the cement slab that lay beneath the bench, Jen sat down cross-legged, facing him. She pulled her locks to one side and wrung hands around them, looking down at her knees.

"I love the way you do that," Nate blurted, laughing as he did so.

His words caught her off guard, and Jen looked quickly up, finding him close to her.

"Do what?" She was afraid she hadn't heard him right.

"I love the way you twist your hair like that."

This time, he wasn't laughing. He wasn't nervous. He was just Nate.

"Really?" she asked in disbelief.

"Yes." His smooth voice spoke again. "Jen...you're..." he paused, as if searching for the right words. "Incredible. Everything about you. You're so kind, and talented, and interesting, and... gorgeous."

Jen could barely breathe, let alone speak, in total astonishment of what she was hearing. She felt a rush of heat flood her cheeks.

"I don't know why it took me so long to realize how I felt." He took her hands in his.

She let the feeling of his touch soak in.

"I know exactly what you mean." She looked into his eyes, and leaned closer to him.

"You do?" A grin that showed his perfect white teeth spread across his face.

"Yes."

"Jen," he whispered, "you are the most amazing person I have ever met. For me...it's only you."

"Me?" she breathed.

"Always. I love you."

"I love you, too."

Nate gently placed his hand on her cheek and pulled her towards him, then closing his eyes, pressed his lips softly against hers. Jen felt the rush of her senses as he kissed her. She breathed him in deeply and leaned in closer. As he kissed her, and pulled her nearer, wrapping his strong arms around her, she was certain she wanted him holding her for the rest of her life.

Acknowledgements

I have been incredibly blessed with many people who have supported me from the moment I said I wanted to write a book, but Cheese, Aimee, and Chuck, you have gone above and beyond. Thank you for your constant prayers and encouragement.

To the friend who inspired a character, Em your willingness to read PhotoJENic so thoroughly and so many times means more to me than I can say. I can only hope I did you justice in capturing the incredible person and friend you are.

Dad-O, the fact that you read PhotoJENic after every edit and constantly encouraged me are just two of many reasons you are the most wonderful and incredible dad in the world.

Keithamator, thank you for knowing me and my book so well that you could create the perfect cover. There is no one I would rather have reading by my side than you. I like you pretty good.

Most of all, though, I thank Moma, for you have not only encouraged me, prayed for me, and taught me, but you gave me a reason to write in the first place.

WENDY BRUENING resides in northeast Ohio with her husband. When she's not writing she spends her free time making music. *PhotoJENic* is her first book.

Made in the USA
Lexington, KY
14 February 2017